THE LEGEND OF SANTOSH CHAUBE

THE INDIAN SANTA CLAUS

SUBHAM THAPA

ISBN
Hardcase 979-8-89544-831-1
Paperback 979-8-89544-547-1

Acknowledgements

To the cherished memory of my father, Ganesh Bahadur Thapa, in whose memory this book finds its soul. To my mother, Indu Thapa, and my brother, Aman Thapa—your love is the foundation of every chapter. And to the one who nurtures my spirit like a Rose in bloom, thank you for being my home.

Contents

"Gather 'round, everyone, and let me tell you a Christmas Content..."

CHAPTER 1

The Awakening

Christmas had cast its magical glow upon the world. Streets were adorned with twinkling lights, trees sparkled with ornaments, and the air was filled with the joyous sounds of carolers. Children laughed, their faces aglow with the spirit of the season, and families gathered, their hearts warmed by the love and togetherness that defined this festive time. From bustling cities to quiet villages, the entire globe seemed wrapped in a blanket of happiness and hope.

Far from the celebrations, hidden deep within the unforgiving peaks of the Himalayas, lay a realm untouched by joy. A snow-covered, craggy peak stood isolated and menacing, crowned by an ancient, long-abandoned tower. Beneath a cloudy sky, its dark silhouette loomed ominously against the towering Himalayas.

A sudden flash of lightning split the sky, illuminating the desolate landscape in a brief, blinding glow. In that fleeting moment, something terrifying was revealed: dark, massive tentacles writhing and coiling around the tower, their sinister forms emerging from the storm-laden clouds. The snow below gleamed like an untouched white blanket, unmarked by any trace of life. There were no footsteps going up or down the hill, yet someone—or something—lived in that tower.

Inside the tower, hidden within the suffocating shadows, a tall, slender figure stood, radiating an ominous aura that chilled the air around him. Each breath he took seemed to draw the darkness closer. Wisps of inky black smoke twisted and swirled at his feet, curling upward in restless, serpentine motions—a manifestation of the evil that pulsed within him." Do you know the greatest weakness of fear and dread?" His voice slithered through the chamber, cold and venomous. "It fades with time."

From the darkness, multiple small eyes blinked open, gleaming bright yellow like those of nocturnal animals. They were kobolds, casting long, eerie shadows on the stone walls. "Ja, Meister," they hissed in unison, their devotion unwavering and terrifying. *("Yes, Master.")*

With a faint, eerie grin, the dark figure issued his chilling command, his words dripping with malice. "The time has come to revive fear and dread. Bring me what I need, or suffer the consequences."

A low, bone-chilling hum resonated from the walls as if the very structure of the tower responded to his power. His eyes gleamed with a wicked, unnatural light, cutting through the darkness like twin blades of malice. The kobolds quickly moved to obey, their glowing eyes vanishing into the shadows as they moved swiftly and silently.

The dark, lanky silhouette of the mysterious figure stood alone, enveloped in suffocating, inky smoke. His breaths were weak and labored, betraying his fading strength. Yet the power he wielded was unmistakable, and his purpose was clear—he would stop at nothing to plunge the world into a living nightmare.

CHAPTER 2

Deck the Halls

Midnight had fallen over the sprawling city of Delhi, blanketing it in profound stillness. The only sounds piercing the silence were the occasional distant barks of dogs echoing through the deserted streets. Christmas was just another day here—there were no twinkling lights, no festive decorations, no signs of celebration. Between the towering buildings, a row of cramped apartments stood in darkness, save for one faintly glowing window on the top floor.

Inside that window was Avnith's room. It was a small, cramped space, barely big enough for the double bed squeezed against one wall. The window, positioned just above a modest study table, overlooked the city below. On the table, a photo frame held a snapshot of happier times: Five-year-old Avnith perched on his father's shoulders, while his mother smiled beside them, holding Avnith's balloons. Beside the photo frame were a table lamp, a pair of headphones, a notebook lay open filled with half-written lyrics, and a Smartphone.

The room was a collage of Avnith's passions. Posters of music legends like Nina Simone, Eric Clapton, and

Kurt Cobain adorned the walls above his bed, each a beacon of his aspirations. Interspersed among the posters were handwritten quotes—some hopeful, others seething with frustration: “Music is my escape,” “Pain is the fuel for my fire,” and “Songs of hope play on repeat, but loneliness still writes my lyrics.” A ukulele leaned against the closed door. From downstairs, Avnith’s voice carried up in a heated argument. “I don’t want to leave my home. I’m staying here!” he shouted, sounding both stubborn and desperate.

Varshikha, his stepmother, responded with equal resolve, “Avnith, it’s enough. The decision has been made. We’re leaving Delhi. Now go to your room.”

A crash echoed through the house—the sound of glass breaking—cutting through the tense air. Footsteps pounded up the stairs, and the door to Avnith’s room flew open before slamming shut with a resounding thud.

Avnith, around eighteen, was tall and skinny, and his face showed his sadness and frustration. His eyes were red-rimmed, the weight of recent events etched into his expression. As he flumped onto his bed, his phone buzzed with messages from friends trying to offer comfort: “Mussoorie is not far, bro!” “Safe journey.” and “ Don’t forget us, Avnith!”

With a heavy sigh, Avnith tossed the phone aside. His gaze landed on the cherished photo of his parents. Tenderly, he picked up the frame, tears spilling over as he traced their smiles with trembling fingers. His voice, barely a whisper, broke the silence. “I miss you, Mom and Dad.”

This small, cramped room was his haven, his home, a place where memories lingered and dreams once flourished. But now, even this refuge was slipping away, a casualty of decisions beyond his control.

As the city of Delhi slept, Avnith's world teetered on the brink of change. The quiet of the night pressed in around him, a stark contrast to the storm raging within.

The early morning air was thick with fog, blanketing the city of Delhi in a shroud of cold and silence. The sun had not yet risen, and everything looked ghostly in the faint light. A car sat parked outside an apartment building, its engine idling softly. The city's usual bustle was muffled, as if the world was holding its breath.

Avnith stood in front of the apartment, his ukulele slung over his shoulder and a backpack hanging from one arm. His gaze was fixed on the house as if trying to imprint every detail into his memory. His eyes, red and tired, mirrored the deep, aching sadness he felt inside.

Behind him, Varshikha, in her mid-thirties, was tall and fair, dressed in a decent black salwar suit. She was helping Danta, a chubby ten-year-old boy wearing a red earflap beanie, load his luggage into the trunk of the car. Danta hops into the car, grinning mischievously, and calls out to Avnith, "Come on, Bhaiya! At this rate, we'll be in Mussoorie by Christmas next year."

Varshikha noticed Avnith's lingering stare and paused, understanding the depth of his emotions. She gently placed her arm on his shoulder, her touch light but supportive. "Time to go," she said softly.

Avnith, still angry and hurt, shrugged off Varshikha's arm and got into the car without saying a word. Varshikha sighed, her heart heavy with the weight of the decisions she had to make. She knew Avnith would be upset with her, but she couldn't leave him alone in the city. It was the only option, but that didn't make it any easier.

She watched him for a moment, hoping that someday he would understand and forgive her. With a final glance at the apartment building, Varshikha closed the trunk and got into the driver's seat. She started the car, and they began their journey, leaving behind the city.

As they drove through the foggy streets, Avnith couldn't help but think about happier times. Each memory was a painful reminder of what he had lost.

The car moved away from the apartment, and the fog covered the last traces of their old life. Avnith stared out the window, tears finally rolling down his face.

After hours of driving, theyfinally reached Mussoorie. The car wound its way through the serpentine mountain roads, with the snow-capped peaks visible in the distance, their white caps glistening under the setting sun.

Varshikha focused intently on the twisting road ahead, her grip on the steering wheel tight with determination. "Focus, Varshikha, it's just a road," she told herself, feeling the weight of responsibility. Beside her, Danta watched a Christmas origin story on YouTube, his face illuminated by the screen's glow. "Mom, did you know that Christmas used to be more for adults, but then it became all about kids because they bring magic and wonder to the holiday"

Varshikha smiled but kept her eyes on the road. "That's interesting, Danta, but right now let me concentrate on driving. It's my first time driving in the mountains."

Danta nodded, turned back to his video, and soon began singing "Deck the Halls" along with the choir on the screen. Avnith, already irritated, told him to stop. Instead, Danta sang louder, right in his brother's face. Tempers flared, and a small fistfight broke out between the brothers.

"Stop it, boys!" Varshikha commanded, her voice stern. She glanced at them through the rearview mirror, her eyes filled with both frustration and concern. The brothers quieted down, exchanging looks, their anger fading for the moment.

Finally, the road led them to a humble cottage nestled among the trees—a small oasis in the vast expanse of wilderness. The cottage was charming, with its quaint architecture and a small garden out front, dusted lightly with snow.

Varshikha's heart raced with nerves as she rang the doorbell. She turned to her kids and whispered, "Be nice guests, okay?" Avnith, uninterested, shrugged while Danta, excited, nodded eagerly.

The door opened, and there stood Abby, a woman who seemed as warm as sunshine after a cloudy day. She was the same age as Varshikha, slim and fair, wearing pants and a sweater and wearing glasses on her nose. Her smile was friendly, and her eyes sparkled with happiness.

"Look who it is!" Abby teased, her voice filled with playful affection. "The city girl in the mountains! How's that for a change?"

Varshikha smiled, the tension easing from her shoulders. "Abby, it's so good to see you!"

They embraced warmly, the hug lingering for a moment as if time had stopped. Abby then turned her attention to the kids, her eyes twinkling with affection.

"Come on in, all of you," she said, waving them inside. "It's freezing out here!"

The group eagerly followed her, the warmth of the house offering a welcome contrast to the chilly mountain air.

Inside Abby's house, Varshikha sat alone in the living room, resting on the sofa. She noticed a chubby toddler doll in a diaper lying still beside her. She looked around the room, which was charming, even though it wasn't decorated for Christmas yet. Her gaze finally settled on a Christmas tree, untouched and undecorated, standing in the corner.

Abby appeared with a tray holding three mugs. ""Here you go, some delicious hot chocolate," she said with a grin. "It's a bestseller at my bakery—keeps the doors swinging open all the time!" She placed the tray on the table and asked, "Where are the kids?"

"They're in the room, just coming," Varshikha replied with a tired smile. She added, "Sorry for informing you on such short notice. My broker went to Karnataka for his sister's wedding and took my house keys with him."

Abby sat down beside Varshikha, her smile warm and reassuring. "Hey, no need to be sorry. You're here, and that's what matters."

Varshikha forced a smile, her mind clearly elsewhere. "Thanks, Abby. It's just... everything happened so fast. One minute, I'm packing up our lives in Delhi, and now we're here in Mussoorie, starting over."

Abby playfully nudged her. "Well, Christmas is all about fresh starts, right? Remember when we tried baking that cake in college? It was a disaster, but we turned it into the best Christmas pudding ever!"

A soft laugh escaped Varshikha. "Yeah, and we ended up with flour everywhere. But this... this isn't just about a cake. It's about uprooting everything, especially for the kids."

Grinning, Abby replied, "True, but you know what they say—Christmas trees need new soil to grow taller. Maybe this move is just what you all need, a little change of scenery to make some new memories."

Varshikha sighed, a hint of relief in her voice. "Maybe you're right. It's just... a lot to handle all at once."

"Hey, it's Christmas," Abby said gently. "If there's ever a time for miracles, it's now. And you're not alone. We've got each other, just like always."

A warm smile spread across Varshikha's face. "Yeah, I hope this Christmas won't be so bad after all."

"Of course not!" Abby winked. "We'll make sure of it. Who knows, maybe we'll even bake another disaster cake for old times' sake."

Varshikha chuckled. "But this time, you're cleaning the floor."

Varshikha smiled slightly, and Abby chuckled, the tension between them easing as they settled into the comfort of their long-standing friendship.

Varshikha sighed, her voice tinged with lingering unease. "But I still wish the hospital staff had given this promotion to someone else. If they had, I wouldn't have to leave Delhi."

Abby picked up her half-knitted sweater and resumed knitting, the rhythmic click of the needles filling the space between them. "How's Avnith dealing with all this?" she asked gently, keeping her tone light.

Varshikha hesitated, her gaze drifting to the untouched Christmas tree in the corner. "He's... struggling. He doesn't say much, but I can tell. It's hard for him to leave everything behind."

Abby nodded, her hands busy with the knitting, but she focused entirely on her friend. "It's a lot for anyone, especially at his age. But he'll adjust,. Kids are resilient"

Varshikha managed a smile and nodded.

The room fell into a comfortable silence.

Avnith and Danta joined Varshikha and Abby in the living room. Danta, brimming with curiosity, asked, "Where are Vini and Aiva Di?"

Abby was about to answer when the door creaked open. "Here are your Vini and Aiva Di!" she exclaimed.

Danta's face lit up as he dashed to the door, wrapping his arms around five-year-old Vini, a small, bubbly girl in a brown kitten-hooded cowl. They giggled with delight, clearly thrilled to see each other.

Behind Vini stood Aiva, who was the same age as Avnith. She had light skin and a slender frame, clad in a light pink knitted sweater, a warm scarf, and an earflap beanie. She was carrying a grocery bag, her demeanour calm and composed.

As Avnith and Aiva locked eyes, the tension in the room became palpable. Their shared past, marked by unresolved emotions and unspoken words, hung between them like a heavy cloud. Their gaze lingered just a moment too long, filled with unvoiced memories and wounds yet to heal. Without a word, Aiva turned abruptly and headed to the kitchen, her footsteps echoing with quiet frustration that resonated through the room. Abby, sensing the brewing storm, quickly followed her. Avnith heard Aiva's raised voice from the kitchen, filled with frustration and anger. "I cannot tolerate him! Just seeing him makes me furious!"

Danta and Varshikha exchanged worried glances before their eyes settled on Avnith, whose fury was palpable as he clenched his jaw tightly. "I told you this wasn't going to end well," he muttered to Varshikha, his voice low yet charged with emotion. Without waiting for a response, he turned abruptly and bolted for his room.

Varshikha's heart sank. She knew Avnith was truly upset now. She hurried after him, hoping to calm him down before things escalated further.

Aiva, fuming with anger, began emptying the grocery bag with deliberate, forceful movements. She took out bottles of strawberry jam and peanut butter from "Prakash and Co." and an Ellora's bread packet, placing them down on the countertop with a thud. Among the groceries lay one of Vini's dolls, a beautiful bisque doll in a pink frock.

Abby entered the kitchen, "What is this behaviour, Aiva? Why are you being so rude?" she asked, her voice a mix of concern and frustration.

Aiva took a deep breath to steady herself. "Mom, I... I just can't face him. Every time I think about fixing things, seeing him just makes me angrier.."

Abby spoke gently. "You two had a fight last year. Every friendship has its ups and downs."

Aiva shook her head vehemently. "But we're not best friends. We just know each other because of you and Varshikha Aunty."

Abby sighed, understanding the deeper roots of Aiva's anger. "I know, but why do you and Avnith have to hold grudges? Just sort this out. This is the best chance since he's here now."

Aiva's face hardened as she relived the painful memory. " I know, and I want to fix things, but..." She paused, unable to bring herself to say the words, but finally, she continued, her voice trembling with hurt and anger, "He said I was adopted. That I was found in the garbage. Tell me, how can I forgive him, Mom?"

Abby felt sad for her daughter. She knew how much Avnith's words had hurt Aiva. "I understand, Aiva. What

Avnith said was wrong. But holding onto grudges is like holding a hot coal—you're the one who gets burned. So, forgive and let go to make your heart feel better.

Aiva looked at her mother, her eyes still angry but also showing pain and doubt. "I don't know if I can, Mom. I'm not that brave."

Abby put a comforting hand on Aiva's shoulder. "It's ok, Take your time".

Aiva nodded slowly, her anger starting to fade as she thought about her mom's words.

Meanwhile, Varshikha opened the door, her expression tense and her mood sour. She found Avnith furiously packing his backpack, tears streaming down his face. "Where are you going?" she asked, trying to keep her voice steady.

"Home," Avnith spat back, his voice cracking with emotion.

Varshikha approached him and gently tried to take his backpack away. "Listen to me," she pleaded.

But Avnith, consumed by anger and sorrow, snatched the backpack away from her. "No, leave me alone!" he cried.

Varshikha took a deep breath. "Apologise to Aiva," she said firmly.

"Why should I? I don't regret what I said. She was the one who tore up the page first," Avnith snapped, his voice trembling with anger and sorrow. "That page was everything to me. You know what was in it."

Varshikha nodded gently. "Yes, I know, but—"

"But nothing!" Avnith interrupted, his frustration boiling over. "It was the only thing that made me feel close to my father and mother. It might not mean much to anyone else, but it was everything to me, and now it's gone." His words hung in the air, thick with the weight of loss.

Varshikha's face showed sympathy, though she tried to stay calm. "I know it was important to you, but holding onto that anger won't help. You need to let it go."

Avnith's face was etched with frustration. "Don't lecture me. Since you came into my life, everything's gone wrong. I lost my father, my city, my friends, and now my home."

Varshikha's tone became more serious. "Watch it…I'm your mom."

Avnith's anger exploded. "You're not my mom, and you never will be!"

Avnith's harsh words pierced Varshikha's heart. Overwhelmed by emotion, she slapped him without thinking. The sharp sound echoed through the room, which fell into stunned silence. Avnith stood there, shocked and tearful, while Varshikha grappled with her own anger and sadness.

Avnith, his eyes blazing with anger, slung his backpack over his shoulder and stormed out of the room. Left alone, Varshikha felt tears streaming down her face. She knew that slapping him had been a mistake and had only deepened the rift. Overcome with regret, she sank to the floor and cried.

Avnith stormed down the stairs, his footsteps heavy with anger. As he reached the middle of the staircase, Abby stood in his path. She looked at him, noticing the redness in his face and the tears in his eyes. "Where are you going?" she asked gently.

Avnith tried to hide his face, his voice trembling. "Step aside. Let me go."

Abby remained firm, her voice calm and soothing. "Avnith, relax. Let's talk." She reached out, attempting to pull his backpack away gently. But Avnith, consumed by his anger and emotions, snatched his backpack back. "Stop it!" he shouted, his frustration caused him to accidentally bump into Abby.

Abby lost her balance, her face flashing with surprise and fear. She screamed as she tumbled backward down the stairs, finally coming to a stop on the floor, unconscious.

Aiva came running at the sound of her mother's scream, followed closely by Danta and Vini. Her eyes widened in horror as she saw her mother lying motionless at the bottom of the stairs.. "Mom!" she cried out, rushing to her side. She glancedup the stairs, her eyes blazing with anger and fear, and saw Avnith standing there, frozen in shock. Varshikha appeared behind Avnith, her eyes widening in horror as she saw Abby at the bottom of the stairs. "Abby!" she gasped, rushing to her friend's side. Avnith stood frozen, his heart pounding and his mind racing. He hadn't meant for this to happen. Tears streamed down his face as he watched the chaos below, grappling with the gravity of the situation.

CHAPTER 3

Santosh Chaube: Indian Santa Claus

In the hospital room, Abby lay on a cot, her leg encased in a thick plaster cast. The sterile smell of antiseptics filled the air, mingling with the faint sound of beeping monitors. She held her phone to her ear, her voice steady but tinged with fatigue.

"I'm all right. It's just a minor fracture," Abby reassured Aiva on the other end of the call. "Listen, I don't think we can make it tonight. We'll come by tomorrow. Take care of everyone, and give kisses to Vini." She ended the call with a sigh, placing the phone on the bedside table.

Abby smiled as Varshikha approached with medicine and a glass of water. "Congratulations, Doctor, you've got your first patient," Abby teased, her eyes twinkling despite the pain.

Varshikha managed a smile, shaking her head. "How can you be so cheerful during tough times? It always amazes me."

Abby leaned back against the pillows, her smile unwavering. "Sadness and happiness are like 2 sides of the same coin. When you have the coin, why just look at one side? Flip it around and enjoy the other side, too."

Varshikha handed Abby a few pills, which Abby took and swallowed with a glass of water. Varshikha then carefully took the empty glass from Abby's hands.

Varshikha felt guilty and said, "I'm really sorry about Avnith."

"Don't worry, I slipped. It's not Avnith's fault," Abby replied, waving it off.

Varshikha's voice was shaking. "He's not a bad kid. He just... hates me. He blames me for his father's death. Sometimes I wish I hadn't been driving that day."

Abby's expression softened as she put a comforting hand on Varshikha's arm. "Hey, it's nobody's fault. It's just happened. "You're his mother; he understands that. Varshikha's eyes are numb. "I don't think Avnith will ever accept me as his mother," she said, her voice full of despair.

Abby squeezed Varshikha's arm gently. "He will," she said softly. "I truly believe that."

Varshikha looked at Abby, searching for reassurance. "It feels like such a long shot. I've tried everything, but it never seems to be enough. I really hope things change."

Abby responded, "As long as you keep hoping, nothing will change. You have to believe in it."

Varshikha looked confused.

Abby explained, "There's a difference between hope and belief. Hope is like a flickering candle—fragile and temporary. Belief is like a steady flame. It's strong and enduring."

Varshikha frowned, trying to understand. "What do you mean?"

Abby smiled gently. "Once, there were two frogs in a pond. One frog hoped the water would stay clean and full of food, just waiting and wishing for the best. The other frog believed that the pond's resources might run out, so it worked hard to find and store food and even cleaned parts of the pond. When a drought came and the water level dropped, the first frog struggled, while the second frog thrived because its belief led it to prepare and adapt."

Varshikha listened closely. "So, you're saying that belief is stronger than hope?"

Abby nodded. "Yes, hope can get you through a tough moment, but belief can carry you through the long haul."

Varshikha smacked her lips in frustration. "I want to believe, but it's so hard."

Abby smiled warmly. "It's okay to feel that way. Belief isn't about having all the answers. It's about having faith in the process and in the possibility. And sometimes, that's enough to help us through."

Back at home, Avnith sat silently on the couch, lost in thought. Danta was next to him, staring at the Christmas tree surrounded by scattered boxes of decorations—fairy lights, stars, bells, caps, balls, socks, and candy canes.

Aiva and Vini were by the tree, unpacking decorations and attempting to arrange them. Vini, unusually quiet, gestured for Danta to join them. Understanding her silent plea, Aiva said, "Danta, come help us decorate!"

Danta looked at Avnith. "Come help us, bhaiya."

Avnith waved a dismissive hand. "I don't have time for this. I don't celebrate Christmas."

Aiva's frustration grew. "It's not just about the decorations. It's about making this time special for everyone."

Avnith scoffed. "Nothing is special."

Aiva's eyes narrowed in irritation. "Why do you have to be like this? It's a chance to make things better."

Avnith's frustration boiled over. "Nothing will get better. And besides, you're the one who keeps making everything worse."

Aiva's anger flared. "We're trying to move on. You're just making it harder. Like always"

Avnith, irritated and fuming, said, "Danta, let's go to the room."

Aiva became adamant, "No, Danta will not go anywhere."

Caught in the middle, Danta was torn, shifting his gaze between Aiva and Avnith as they argued heatedly. Uncertain whether to stay or leave, his dilemma was palpable. Just then, Vini shouted, "Stop!" The room fell silent. She looked at Avnith and said, "It's Christmas, Bhaiya. If we don't decorate the Christmas tree, Santa won't come."

Avnith's smirk widened. "Vini, didn't your sister tell you? There's no such thing as Santa Claus. He's not real."

Vini's eyes filled with shock and tears, her belief wavering. "Avnith Bhaiya, you're lying... Santa is real."

Avnith shrugged dismissively, his expression cold. "Stay up all night and see if Santa really comes to give you a gift or not." With a final smirk, he turned and left the room.

Little Vini turned to Aiva, her eyes glistening with tears. "Didi, Santa is real, right?"

Aiva knelt down and wrapped her arms around her little sister, her voice tender and reassuring. "Santa is real, Vini. Don't listen to Avnith Bhaiya."

Sobbing, Vini clung to Aiva, her innocence visibly shaken. She gazed up at the star atop the Christmas tree, her thoughts uncertain.

Later that night, Avnith sat on the terrace wall, gazing up at the full moon and the stars that lit up the sky, lost in thought.. He strummed his ukulele softly, trying to calm his troubled mind. He sang his father's song, filling the night air, but it was interrupted when the terrace door creaked open.

Aiva appeared, wrapped in a shawl. Her presence was unexpected but not unwelcome. She stood beside him, and for a moment, they both remained silent, the awkwardness between them hanging in the air.

Finally, Avnith broke the silence. "What do you want?"

Aiva's voice was steady but tinged with frustration. "This is my home. I can go wherever I want. Why do you always talk so rudely?"

Avnith didn't respond, his fingers strumming the ukulele absentmindedly. For a moment, he and Aiva remained silent. Finally, Avnith sighed deeply, his gaze still fixed on the stars. "Vini," he said quietly, "is she alright?" His words carried the weight of regret.

Aiva reassured him with a small smile,. "Yeah, she'll be fine. She is just 5; she doesn't hold onto grudges for long like us."

They fell silent once more. Aiva spoke again, her voice quieter. "You know," she began, "every Christmas, Vini writes her wish to Santa and puts it in a sock. Mom and I read it to make sure we get her whatever she asks for. When she finds her wish come true the next morning, it makes us really happy. For us, Christmas is all about making Vini happy. But this year, she didn't wish for anything. She just cried and went to sleep."

Avnith kept his gaze fixed on the stars, avoiding eye contact. There was a look of guilt in his eyes, but he said nothing.

They stood in silence again. Aiva glanced at her wristwatch and saw that it was midnight. "By the way," she said softly, "Merry Christmas."

Avnith remained silent, his gaze fixed on the stars. His eyes, filled with guilt and remorse, betrayed the heavy burden of having hurt little Vini. Aiva gave him one last, uncertain glance before turning to leave, but their moment was interrupted by an unexpected sound that shattered the quiet of the terrace – a strange, eerie "DING-A-LING!" like the chime of a bell.

Avnith and Aiva exchanged startled glances, their senses on high alert as the jingling sound seemed to come from all directions, echoing through the night air, "DING-A-LING! DING-A-LING!"

Avnith, scanning the surroundings with wide eyes, quipped nervously, "You didn't tell me your place is haunted."

Aiva, equally puzzled, replied, "I didn't know either."

The jingling grew louder, like a melody coming from the sky. Avnith pointed up, his voice full of surprise. "Look! What is that?"

A dark silhouette approached rapidly, its form indistinct yet unsettling as it closed in on the terrace. With a loud thud, it collided with the terrace wall and headed fast toward Avnith and Aiva as if it were about to hit them. Avnith and Aiva closed their eyes in fear and screamed, but nothing struck them.

Slowly, they opened their eyes and stood frozen in shock. Before them were two reindeer, their hooves clattering against the floor. The creatures sneezed, emitting puffs of fog into the chilly air.

Both Avnith and Aiva instinctively stepped back, and their astonishment mingled with disbelief.

"Tell me this isn't real," Aiva whispered urgently.

Avnith, equally bewildered, affirmed, "It's real."

The eight reindeer, harnessed with elaborate straps decorated with jingling bells, pulled a massive red carriage that combined the charm of a snowmobile with the intricacy of a steampunk aircraft. The carriage's shiny red surface and brass fittings glinted in the moonlight. It featured intricate gears and steam pipes, with ornate blades ready to glide over snow, ice, and even into the sky. The reindeers' harnesses sparkled with twinkling bells that chimed softly with each movement.

Suddenly, someone leaps from the carriage and lands on the ground—it's Santa Claus himself. He is a towering figure with a white beard and an unexpectedly serious expression. Clad in a traditional red robe trimmed with black fur, a plaid shirt, dhoti-style pants, a black belt, and sturdy boots, he also sports distinctive steampunk goggles and a tilaka on his forehead. Despite his impressive appearance, this Santa looks more middle-aged than the jolly old man most people expect.

"HO! HO! HO!" Santa's greeting sounded weak and disinterested, as if he barely wanted to say it. Suddenly, he was overtaken by a fit of coughing. He fumbled inside his robe, pulling out a small flask and taking a quick swig before finally turning to face Avnith and Aiva.

"Christmas ki hardik shubhkamnaye!" he exclaimed, his cheer sounding hollow and almost forced.

Aiva and Avnith exchanged confused glances. "What?!" they asked in unison.

Santa rolled his eyes and let out a tired sigh. "Merry Christmas, Avnith and Aiva," he corrected, sounding far less jolly.

Aiva stared, still wide-eyed with disbelief. "Are you... real?" she asked, her voice filled with awe.

Santa let out a yawn, clearly unimpressed. "You can pull my beard if you don't believe it, Aiva."

Avnith, still grappling with the surreal scene unfolding before him, voiced the question on his mind, "How do you know our names?"

Santa, unfazed by their skepticism, explained in irritation, "I follow you guys on social media. Of course, I'm Santa Claus – I know everyone's names. Now, don't waste my time. Where's Vini?."

Avnith and Aiva were confused but more shocked to see a weird, arrogant, and rude Santa Claus.

Aiva's curiosity is piqued, but her suspicion lingers. "Wait. Why do you want to see Vini?"

Avnith, echoing her uncertainty, added, "Yeah, what's going on?"

Santa rolled his eyes, clearly annoyed by having to explain. He pointed at Avnith. "Ask him."

Avnith, confused, asked, "Me?"

Santa Claus leaned toward him, his presence dominating. "It's all because of you. If you hadn't broken Vini's heart, I wouldn't be here."

Avnith opened his mouth to speak, but Santa silenced him with a finger held to his lips. "Zip it, boy."

Aiva glanced at Avnith with a gentle look. "You broke Vini's heart."

Avnith's guilt resurfaced, and he tried to defend himself, addressing Santa. "How was I supposed to know Santa Claus is real? I'm Hindu." Turning to Aiva, he added, "And you didn't believe in him either."

Aiva, stepping back from the blame, retorted, "Don't put that on me."

Santa, standing tall over Avnith, said, "There's a reason why we keep our existence hidden, and don't be discriminatory – even Hindus celebrate Christmas these days. Now, stop wasting my time. I have gifts to deliver. I don't want to lose part of my salary for being late. So, I'm going to see Vini myself. Thank you, and shut up."

With that, Santa descended the terrace stairs, Avnith and Aiva trailing behind, their minds reeling with questions.

Aiva, clearing her doubts and seeking answers, asked, "Santa, you can't be here just because Vini cried and is hurt. What's really going on?"

Avnith, equally eager for answers, pressed further. "Yeah, tell us."

Santa, uninterested, muttered, "Oh my Nicholas! I hate kids."

Avnith and Aiva's eyes widened in shock. Santa hated kids? Avnith nervously asked, "Are you really Santa Claus?"

Santa, feeling hurt by the doubt, immediately turned back to them. "I'm just asking," Avnith quickly added.

Santa reached into his magical pocket, burying his entire arm inside. As he searched, his face contorted with concentration. A cacophony of sounds erupted from within: clinking, the shattering of glass, and even the plaintive meowing of a cat named Cutie Pie, who was biting Santa's hand and making him yelp in surprise.

"Watch out, Cutie Pie!" Santa exclaimed.

"Wow," Avnith gasped while Aiva marveled at the sheer spectacle unfolding before them.

Finally successful in his quest within the magical pocket, Santa retrieved an object that he held out to Avnith and Aiva, extending his arm with a flourish. Resting on his palm was a miniature book.

Avnith and Aiva stared in wonder at the book, their disbelief evident. "What is this?" they questioned simultaneously.

Santa, smirking as he loved showing off magic to humans, whistled. The miniature book expanded before their eyes, growing larger until it was no longer miniature at all. Santa balanced the ancient tome delicately between his hands, its aged red leather cover cracked and weathered, bearing intricate designs of tiny Christmas trees and delicate snowflakes gently falling.

Avnith and Aiva were fascinated as they saw the cover with the title: "STRICT RULES AND REGULATIONS FOR SANTA CLAUS."

Santa, now wearing glasses perched on his nose, flipped through the book until he found the passage he sought. He began to explain, "Children of age 5 or under who truly believe in Santa Claus – a pure soul and believer – it's our duty as Santa to fulfil their Christmas wishes at any cost. They are our true believers the reason Christmas magic still thrives. If we do not fulfill their wish, then under the SPC 186, we will be punished...." He stopped, coughing and clearing his throat, not wanting to go into the details of the punishment.

Santa, feeling the heavy burden on his shoulders, said with irritation, "Vini wished – 'If Santa Claus is real, then she wanted to see him. If I don't show up, she'll never celebrate Christmas again.' So here I am, doing my job."

Aiva and Avnith tried to process it all Santa continued, "Honestly, I'm tired of delivering gifts every year. I'd rather have a desk job. Vini's wish is a once-in-a-lifetime chance for me to get a promotion and a better salary." He closed his book and stuffed it back into his magical pocket. "Now, take me to Vini."

Moments later, Santa watched Vini sleep peacefully, feeling bored. Aiva positioned herself next to Vini's bed, gently swaying and softly whispering words to rouse her from slumber. "Vini, wake up. Look, Santa is here for you."

Vini, still half-asleep, stirred and slowly opened her eyes, greeted by the presence of Santa Claus. She rubbed her lazy eyes and let out a sleepy yawn.

Santa, with a touch of reluctance, gently lifted Vini into his arms and blew softly. A frosty blue wind, carrying tiny snowflakes, swirled around her. Her hair fluttered as though she were standing in a gentle breeze, and Santa's magical breath created a wintry aura around her. Gradually, Vini woke up, fully alert.

Vini's eyes sparkled with awe and joy. Filled with enchantment, she gazed up at Santa Claus with wide eyes and asked, her voice brimming with wonder, "Are you really Santa?"

Santa, bored, responded, "You can pull my beard if you don't believe."

Embracing the magic of the moment, Vini giggled with delight and playfully tugged at Santa's beard. Santa let out an unexpected groan of pain. He murmured to himself in irritation, "I hate kids." Avnith and Aiva swiftly intervened.

Santa, recovering from the playful tugging, adjusted his jaw while Avnith peered over his shoulder with a concerned expression.

"Santa, are you all right?" Avnith asked.

Santa, frustrated, responded, "First, grow a beard, kid, and then ask me that."

Overjoyed, Vini leaned forward to hug Santa, her heart filled with belief and joy. "I knew you were real. Merry Christmas, Santa"

Santa, unaccustomed to such spontaneous affection from children, felt a bit awkward. He hesitated for a moment before gently patting Vini's back with his finger, unsure of how to respond.

Just then, a scream echoed from the terrace, startling everyone and filling them with concern. Aiva was quickly asked, "What was that?"

Santa sensed trouble and remarked, "Smells like trouble."

Avnith, equally concerned, added, "It's Danta."

Avnith, Aiva, Vini, and Santa rushed towards the terrace, their hearts pounding with worry and confusion. They opened the door and witnessed a surreal sight: the sleigh lifting off into the sky, with Danta perilously hanging from it, calling out for help, "Bhai, help me!!"

Danta's eyes were wide with fear as he looked down at the terrace disappearing beneath him, carried away into the dark clouds by Santa's sleigh.

Santa stood transfixed, his gaze locked on the sleigh as it disappeared into the clouds. And just like that, it was gone. His brows furrowed in concern as he muttered to himself, "This shouldn't be happening..."

Avnith, grappling with a torrent of emotions ranging from fear to frustration, turned to Santa desperately, pleading for action. "Santa, your deer—they took my brother. Please, do something!"

Santa, regaining his composure, corrected Avnith, "First of all, they are reindeer, not deer. And I highly doubt they kidnapped Danta. There must be some mistake. Perhaps Danta got himself into this."

Avnith vehemently defended his brother's character, shaking his head. "No way. Danta wouldn't do something like this."

Aiva, standing close behind Santa, chimed in, her voice laced with concern. "Santa, we need to do something."

Santa, frustrated and irritated, exclaimed, "Damn it. I can't even send an emergency signal back to the Santa Claus Base now."

Aiva, her curiosity piqued by the mention of a "base," pressed Santa for more information. "What do you mean by 'Santa Claus Base'? Like a military base?"

Santa yelled at Aiva. "Yes! All the Santas are trained there. Any more questions, Einstein?"

Avnith, still trying to wrap his head around the revelations, couldn't help but ask, "Hold on, there are multiple Santas? How many?"

Santa turned to Avnith and yelled, "One Santa Claus per country, Bachchan Sahab."

Aiva and Avnith exchanged stunned glances, absorbing the magnitude of this revelation. Their minds raced with questions about the original Santa Claus, Saint Nicholas.

"And Saint Nicholas?" Aiva asked. "Where is he?"

Santa grabbed his forehead in tension. "Old Saint Nick? He's chilling in his grand palace, enjoying his retirement after centuries of delivering gifts, and I'm here doing my duty."

Avnith's sense of bewilderment deepened. "So, who are you then?"

Santa took a deep sigh. "I am Santosh Chaube, one and only Indian Santa Claus. The most awesome, the most amazing—hashtag OP!"

As the weight of the situation settled upon them, Aiva and Avnith couldn't help but express their dismay with a shared exclamation, "Oh, fuck!"

Vini, ever the innocent inquisitor, interrupted with her curiosity, "What does 'fuck' mean?"

Santa, Avnith, and Aiva exchanged a brief, bewildered glance, unsure of how to address Vini's question amidst the chaos of Danta's disappearance.

Santa looked up at the sky, his brow furrowing as he refocused on the urgent task at hand. "I need to find my sleigh ASAP."

Avnith added, "And my brother."

Santa nodded reluctantly. "Yes, I need to find my sleigh and your brother. Otherwise, I'll lose my job and my promotion, and I can't afford that." He paused dramatically, clearly grasping the seriousness of the situation. But then, as if the gravity of the moment had slipped his mind, Santa suddenly blurted out, "I'm hungry."

Aiva and Avnith exchanged confused glances, puzzled by this peculiar Indian Santa Claus. Meanwhile, little Vini gazed at Santa with adoring eyes, which made him feel slightly nervous and awkward.

CHAPTER 4

The Misadventure Begins

Santa and Avnith slouched on the couch, surrounded by crumpled chip packets, Santa was lost in his chips, reaching into the bags and munching away with a focused enthusiasm. Avnith watched him, astonished. Santa told him, "Food helps me think and keeps me calm."

Nearby, Aiva paced restlessly, her face showing worry and impatience.

Unable to contain her anxiety any longer, Aiva blurted out, "Can you guys focus? Danta is missing!" "We have to find him before sunrise; otherwise, our mom—well, I don't know how she'll handle it."

Avnith replied dismissively, "What can I do if Indian Santa here isn't doing anything?"

Aiva stopped pacing, her eyes locking onto Santa. "So, do you have any plan ?"

With a mouthful of chips, Santa shook his head slightly, his lips pursed shut. "Nah, still thinking."

Aiva couldn't resist a sarcastic comeback, "Great."

Vini walked in, her small frame weighed down by a deep sense of loss. She stood next to Aiva, her voice trembling as she said, "I can't find Bholu and Chinya."

Aiva offered a reassuring tone, "Look carefully, Vini. They might be around here somewhere."

Santa, with a few chip crumbs stuck in his beard, glanced at Vini and said urgently, "Guys, I think I know who took my sleigh and kidnapped Danta."

Aiva and Avnith immediately asked in unison, "Who?"

Santa replied with a grim expression, "Kobold. Mutt-fracker."

Vini, Avnith, and Aiva exchanged looks of surprise and confusion, their faces mirroring the collective bewilderment of the moment.

Always ready with questions, Aiva chimed in, "What on earth is Kobold?"

High above the world, Santa's stolen sleigh hurtled forward like a blazing comet, trailing a shimmering path of magical dust behind it. Inside the carriage, Danta, bound and gagged, struggled futilely against his restraints. His eyes were wide with fear and desperation as he writhed, each attempt to free himself meeting with helpless resistance.

Across from him sat Bholu, Vini's chubby toddler doll with movable plastic limbs. Though he looked innocent, Bholu wore a wide grin and slapped Danta playfully, saying, "Stop moving."

Nearby, Chinya, a delicate bisque toddler doll, laughed softly. "Foolish humans," she said, her voice dripping with disdain. She held the reins of the sleigh and stared ahead with intense, calculating focus.

Chinya addressed Bholu with an unsettling calmness in her voice. "We've accomplished what countless kobolds couldn't. Darksant will reward us for this."

"No more serving him," Bholu declared, his voice tinged with a newfound sense of liberation.

"And no more Christmas," Chinya affirmed, her tone resolute and unwavering.

Filled with fervent excitement, they both shouted in unison, "Freiheit!"—the word for freedom echoing with a dark promise of what was to come.

Chinya's gaze was fixed on the sleek dashboard of the sleigh, a maze of flight instruments and controls that beckoned for her command. Among the array of dials and gauges, one element stood out starkly—a menacing red button positioned at the center of the dashboard. Her plastic fingers hovered above it, a sense of purpose in her mechanical movements as she prepared to activate their audacious plan.

With a determined nod, Chinya pressed the red button. Below the sleigh, the hidden launch slot sprang open, gears whirring as the mechanism came to life. She reached for the vintage-looking gear stick, her small hands grasping it with certainty. As she pulled it, the sleigh shuddered, and the air crackled with energy.

In a dazzling display of lights and colors, two basketball-sized spheres shot out from the missile launcher with a thunderous "POW!" The spheres glowed in radiant hues of red and green, leaving shimmering trails in their wake. As they streaked toward the heavens, they collided, creating an awe-inspiring explosion of light.

A massive hyperdrive teleport gate formed between the swirling rings of Looney Tunes-esque circles and a vortex swirling ominously in the sky. The gate stretched wide, its surface rippling like liquid energy, beckoning them forward. The sleigh hummed with anticipation, ready to pass through the kaleidoscopic portal that shimmered with every color imaginable.

The sleigh charged into the portal with unparalleled speed, its form blurring into a streak of light as it disappeared into the swirling gateway. The portal closed behind it with a soft, resonating hum, leaving only traces of shimmering magical particles that twinkled in the night sky.

For a moment, everything was still. The night, wrapped in winter's quiet chill, seemed to hold its breath.

Back in the Abby house, Santa, Avnith, and Vini lay flat on the floor, their faces pressed against the ground as they peered into the dark space beneath the bed. Aiva stood nearby, observing their search with a mix of curiosity and concern. Santa adjusted his steampunk glasses, squinting into the shadowy void.

Aiva, her patience wearing thin, asked once more, "What exactly is a Kobold?"

Santa began, "A Kobold is a type of house spirit..."

Vini, her eyes wide with curiosity, asked, "What's a house spirit?"

Santa explained, "They are creatures from German stories. They're tricky and hard to catch. St. Nick has tried many times to control them, but they just keep spreading their trouble everywhere." Vini's eyes lit up with interest.

Aiva, always analytical, added her own query, "What do they do?"

With a deliberate effort, Santa began to rise from his prone position, propping himself on his knees while using the bed for support. Avnith and Vini followed suit, their curiosity piqued.

"Have you ever experienced something like this?" Santa's voice took on a contemplative tone, drawing them into his narrative. "Have you ever left something in one place, only to find it mysteriously moved somewhere else? Or felt a presence in the room when you were alone, hearing strange noises in the dead of night, like rapid footsteps on the terrace when everyone else is fast asleep?"

Avnith nodded fervently, his excitement palpable, "Yes, many times!"

Aiva nodded in agreement, "Me too."

Santa smiled knowingly, "That, my friends, is a Kobold."

Santa got back into action, swiftly rummaging through Aiva and Vini's clothes in the cupboard, searching with urgency

"Kobolds look like small goblins or hobgoblins," he explained, his voice muffled as he rummaged through the clothes. "They usually prefer to live in human homes, often disguising themselves as dolls or toys."

Santa stood on his tiptoes to reach the higher shelves. "Kobolds are known troublemakers," he continued, his voice blending amusement with caution. "They delight in causing mischief and chaos, playing tricks that disrupt the peace of a house."

Aiva's voice interjected, "That's bizarre."

In the next room, Santa and the children gathered around the toilet seat. Santa, still sporting his steampunk glasses, carefully lifted the commode seat and peered inside. His eyes, magnified by the glasses, scanned the space with a mix of curiosity and determination.

Vini, ever curious, asked innocently, "Are Chinya and Bholu kobolds too?"

Santa nodded knowingly, a twinkle in his eye, "Yes, they are."

He continued searching inside the refrigerator, carefully checking its contents. Santa found a jar of jam, opened it, and tasted a bit with his finger. "Holy Nick," he said, enjoying the flavour. He then put the jar into his magic pocket.

Aiva, her patience wearing thin, questioned Santa, "Santa, we understand. But what exactly are you searching for?"

Santa paused, his expression thoughtful, "Ah, that's the question, isn't it? I'm looking for a doorway."

Avnith looked puzzled, "A doorway? What's that?"

Aiva, grasping Santa's meaning, suggested, "You mean a portal?"

Santa shook his head firmly. "No, a doorway."

Aiva corrected him, "Yes, but scientifically, it's called a portal."

Santa groaned in irritation. "I don't care what science says; I believe in magic."

All of a sudden, Vini screamed, "Didi!" Aiva and Avnith spun around, their hearts pounding with fear and urgency. Santa stayed where he was, rolling his eyes in frustration and trying to calm himself.

"What happened, Vini?" Aiva's voice was filled with concern as she knelt beside her, gently resting a hand on her shoulder.

"I saw lights under the couch," she exclaimed, her eyes wide with wonder

Avnith and Aiva exchanged a worried glance. "Light?"

Santa's expression shifted as he processed her words. "Lights? Ah, of course," he murmured, a spark of realisation dawning in his eyes. "Children under the age of 5 can see doorway."

With a swift motion, Santa flipped the couch over. Adjusting his steampunk glasses, he peered closely at the bottom of the couch, where a soft, ethereal glow radiated in a circle. His eyes widened in amazement as the light shimmered gently, revealing the hidden magic beneath.

"Oh, my stars," Santa breathed, his voice filled with awe.

Avnith and Aiva exchanged puzzled glances, unable to see anything out of the ordinary.

"What are you seeing, Santa?" Aiva asked, her voice tinged with scepticism.

Santa handed his steampunk goggles to Aiva.

Aiva hesitated for a moment before putting on the goggles. The world around her shifted, revealing a mesmerising sight of swirling blue energy beneath the couch. Her eyes widened in disbelief, and she gasped softly.

"Whoa," she whispered, her voice tinged with wonder. "I can see it."

Santa's voice was firm as he pointed to the doorway. "This is the way."

Avnith's face was a mask of concern. "Can we save Danta through this?"

Santa's shoulders sagged slightly. "I don't know."

Avnith's frustration was palpable. "What do you mean you don't know? You're Santa!"

Santa met Avnith's gaze with a tired look. "I'm not St. Nicholas. I'm Santosh Chaube. And don't talk to me like this. This mess started because of you."

Avnith's anger was evident, but he held his tongue.

Santa continued with resolve. "I really hope this doorway leads us to Danta. It's the only chance we've got."

Aiva's fear was clear. "But it's dangerous?"

Santa's demeanour grew stern. "So what? I'm not going alone. You both are coming with me."

Avnith, still simmering with frustration, prepared to follow. Aiva, however, hesitated. "What about Vini? We can't risk her life?"

Just then, a scream of excitement pierced the air. They all turned in horror to see Vini jumping into the glowing portal and disappearing from sight.

Santa's face twisted with fury and exasperation. "I HATE KIDS!"

Together, they stood before the pulsating portal beneath the couch. Santa led the way, his silhouette merging with the glowing blue entrance as he disappeared into the unknown. Avnith followed swiftly, leaping into the portal and vanishing from sight.

Aiva, left alone on the threshold, watched in disbelief. Her heart pounded with a mix of fear and determination. She adjusted Santa's steampunk glasses, squinting at the pulsating portal. With a deep breath, she jumped into the portal.

The moment Aiva entered, she was plunged into a slide of glowing, ethereal blue. Her screams echoed through the swirling currents of the portal as she hurtled downward. The walls of the tunnel pulsed and shimmered around her, casting eerie, dancing shadows in the dim light.

As Aiva continued her descent, the tunnel grew darker and darker, the once-vibrant blue glow fading into obscurity. The air around her grew heavy, and the tunnel seemed to shrink with each passing moment, stretching into an endless abyss. The overwhelming sensations pressed in on her, and her vision blurred, her consciousness slipping away as darkness enveloped her.

The last thing she glimpsed was a fleeting swirl of colors and distant echoes before everything faded into unconsciousness.

CHAPTER 5

The Darksant

Aiva lay unconscious on the cold stone floor, her body limp and motionless. Avnith and Vini knelt beside her, their faces etched with worry and fear.

"Didi, wake up," Vini urged, gently shaking her shoulder. Her voice trembled as she called out again, "Didi, please wake up."

Santa, observing the scene with disinterest, reached into his magical pocket and pulled out a flask.

He unscrewed the cap, and a faint, greenish glow emanated from within.

"Step aside," Santa instructed softly. Avnith and Vini moved back slightly, their eyes fixed on Santa's actions.

Santa poured a small amount of the greenish liquid into his palm. The liquid shimmered with an otherworldly light.. He leaned over Aiva and carefully sprinkled the liquid onto her face.

The effect was immediate. Aiva's eyelids fluttered, and she gasped, sitting up with a jolt. Vini threw her arms around her sister, her small frame shaking with relief.

Santa capped the flask and returned it to his pocket. Avnith's eyes darted around wildly as he tried to make sense of his surroundings. "Where are we?" he exclaimed, his voice tinged with confusion and fear.

The 4 of them stood on a raised platform, their breaths softly echoing in the eerie quiet. They were surrounded by a large, curved medieval wall with thirteen dark tunnels spread out across it like gaping mouths. Avnith, Santa, Aiva, and Vini were at the centre, feeling the heavy weight of uncertainty.

In front of them, a huge, creepy hallway stretched into the darkness. The hallway was flanked by massive columns that seemed to reach up into the shadows. Medieval wall sconces lined the corridor, but there were no flames to light their way.

Santa looked around with a deep furrow in his brow. The confusion was evident in his eyes as he tried to make sense of their surroundings. "Where are we?" he muttered under his breath, more to himself than to anyone else.

The darkness ahead was so thick and heavy that it seemed to swallow all light and hope. It felt like the air around them was getting thicker, making it hard to breathe and think.

Vini held onto Santa's hand tightly, clearly frightened. Her voice was small and shaky as she said, "I'm scared," her eyes searching for any sign of comfort. Santa, unsure of how to respond, felt uncomfortable and hoped she would let go of his hand.

Avnith, usually so strong, admitted, "This time, even I'm scared too."

Aiva, still trying to steady herself after waking up in such an unsettling place, was sweating heavily and struggling to stay calm.

All of a sudden, a voice pierced the thick silence. "Avnith! Help!" It was Danta, his tone desperate and pleading.

The children immediately looked around, their eyes wide with shock and hope. Avnith's heart raced as he scanned the shadows, seeking the source of the cry. His gaze fell upon a faint movement deep within the hallway.

"There!" he shouted, pointing toward a shadowy figure in the distance. Without hesitation, he began to walk down the platform.

Santa reached out, his voice urgent, "Hey! We don't know what's out there!"

But Avnith, determined to save his brother, shook off Santa's hand. "You're not going to do anything, but I have to do something," he said, his tone resolute.

Santa, irritated, snapped, "Fine! You never listen to adults. Go on, then! I hope you see a ghost or something."

"Bhaiya, help me!" Danta's cry echoed again.

"Avnith, wait!" Santa called out, this time reaching for his arm. But before he could grab Avnith's arm, a sudden sharp, cold vapor escaped his mouth, forming a visible puff in the freezing air. The temperature had dropped suddenly, an icy chill gripping them all. Avnith halted mid-step, feeling the biting cold seep into his skin. His breath came out in frosty clouds, and the air around him thickened, the freezing silence amplifying Danta's distant pleas for help.

Vini and Aiva shivered, their breath visible in the freezing air. "It's so cold," Vini whispered, her voice trembling. Aiva wrapped her arms around Vini.

Santa's concern deepened, and a flicker of fear crossed his usually calm features. "This isn't right," he muttered, glancing warily at the encroaching darkness.

"Avnith, listen to me," Santa scolded. "We need to stay together."

Suddenly, dark, smoke-like tentacles lashed out with violent speed, striking Santa with tremendous force. He was flung across the room, crashing into the wall with a loud thud before crumpling to the ground, dazed and gasping for breath. Avnith, Aiva, and Vini stood frozen, their hearts pounding in their chests, eyes wide with fear as the swirling black tentacles hovered menacingly above them. The eerie shadows danced across the cold stone walls, growing larger with each sinister movement, amplifying the terror that now gripped the group.

Just as their fear peaked, the tentacles drifted back into the dark hallway and vanished.

Suddenly, dim flames flickered to life in the sconces along the walls, casting a faint, flickering light that pushed back the oppressive darkness. The room, once cloaked in shadow, revealed a long hallway stretching out before them, leading toward a platform at the far end. At the center of the platform stood a tall, slender figure, its dark form cloaked in shadow yet unmistakably imposing. The faint glow of the flames cast eerie highlights on the figure, which stood before a grand, ominous throne, watching them in silence, its presence filling the space with dread.

A creepy laugh echoed through the chamber, sending chills down Santa's and the children's spines.. "Finally, you're here, Santa," the figure rasped, coughing as if trying to hold back a sinister laugh.

Santa, rose to his feet. "Who are you?" he demanded, his voice steady despite the terror creeping into his heart.

The dark figure moved slightly, and there was a touch of anger in its voice. "Have I been forgotten in Santa's Land? Don't you know who I am? I'm the one who will end Christmas." Santa rolled his eyes and sighed in frustration. "Look, whoever you are, don't make things harder for yourself. I really don't want to be a hero here."

The dark figure let out an evil laugh that echoed through the large hall. "Good, then you'll die peacefully," it said.

Dark smoke began to swirl around the menacing figure, gradually enveloping him until he was nothing but a shadowy mist. The smoke coalesced, drifting from his throne to settle ominously before Santa, Avnith, Aiva, and Vini. As the smoke dissipated, the figure emerged in full.

The figure before them was an abomination. His sickly pale skin stretched tight over a skeletal frame, giving him an eerie, deathly appearance. He wore no hat, and long, thin strands of decayed hair dangled from his scalp. His right sleeve was missing, revealing a bony, lifeless arm. His face was a horror show: the bones beneath the skin were nearly visible, his eye sockets so deep that only hollow cavities remained. The suit, once vibrant in green and white, had faded into tattered rags, dirty and torn.

The sheer malevolence radiating from him was palpable. The kids screamed in terror, while Santa's eyes widened in horror as he recognized the evil presence standing before them.

Dark smoke began to swirl around the evil figure's wrist, gradually shaping into a menacing longsword. With each step he took towards Santa and the kids, the oppressive weight of his presence filled them with an overwhelming sense of fear and hopelessness. The air grew colder, and the hallway seemed to shrink under his dark, foreboding aura. Santa positioned himself defensively as his gaze fixed on the dark figure. The dark figure was now fully revealed as he grinned wickedly. "Prepare to meet your end, Santa. Darksant is here."

The children huddled together, their fear palpable as Darksant advanced, his dark longsword trailing wisps of shadowy smoke, like frost creeping from a block of ice. The blade, pitch black and devoid of any gleam, seemed to absorb the light around it.

. Santa sprang into action immediately. He reached into his pocket and pulled out a small spruce twig. As he held it aloft, a white, snowy light enveloped it, transforming it into a gleaming talwar, an elegant Indian sword.

With a clash that echoed through the vast chamber, Santa blocked Darksant's vicious attack, the two swords meeting with a shower of sparks. In a fluid motion, Santa delivered a powerful punch to Darksant, sending him sliding back across the stone floor. Aiva, Avnith, and Vini watched in awe, their eyes wide as they saw Santa's formidable combat skills in action.

Darksant regained his footing, a twisted smile spreading across his withered face. "Finally, a worthy opponent," he hissed, his voice dripping with dark delight.

Santa and Darksant clashed in a fierce sword duel, their blades ringing through the chamber like a symphony of steel. Santa's moves were precise and powerful, while Darksant's strikes, though swift, lacked strength. Santa pressed the attack, driving Darksant back with each blow.

With a guttural growl, Darksant realised he was losing ground. He turned into a swirling mass of dark smoke, retreating swiftly across the stone floor. The smoke coalesced near the throne, settling into Darksant's ominous form once more. Revealed before him, trembling and tear-streaked, was Danta.

"Danta!" Avnith cried, his voice breaking with fear and desperation.

Avnith made a move toward his brother, but Santa's strong hand gripped his arm, holding him back. "No, stay here," Santa commanded, his eyes never leaving Darksant.

"Leave Danta alone!" Aiva and Vini shouted, their voices echoing in the vast, dark hall.

Santa's talwar shimmered, transforming back into a simple spruce twig. He tucked it into his pocket and faced Darksant with a steely resolve. "Let's be calm and talk," Santa said, his voice firm yet diplomatic.

Darksant's lips twisted into a sinister smile. "Now you're talking," he sneered.

Santa took a deep breath. "What do you want for Danta's release?"

Darksant's eyes glittered with malice. "Your robe and hat. Give them to me, and I'll release the boy."

"No!" Santa's refusal was immediate and resolute, causing the children to look at him in shock and confusion.

"Santa, please, just give him what he wants!" Avnith pleaded. "It's just a robe and hat."

"Yeah, it's no big deal!" Vini echoed, tears streaming down her face.

"You don't understand," Santa said, his voice heavy with gravity. "The robe and hat are more than just clothing."

Darksant chuckled. Black smoke swirled around his hand, forming a small, gleaming knife. He placed it against Danta's throat, causing the boy to cry out in terror.

"No!" Avnith, Aiva, and Vini screamed in unison, their voices filled with horror and urgency.

Santa was stuck in a terrible situation, his mind racing for a way out. Darksant pressed the knife closer to Danta's skin, making the boy cry even more. Santa muttered to himself in frustration, "I'm going to lose my job. Kids! Ugh!"

He glared at Avnith, his anger clear. "You! The cause of all this trouble!" Santa shouted, blaming Avnith for the mess they were in.

Reluctantly, Santa shouted, "Fine! I'll give you my robe and hat." His voice was filled with frustration as he prepared to give up his important items.

Darksant's smile widened, victorious. "Good choice, Santa."

Santa slowly approached them. His eyes locked onto the Darksant holding the Danta hostage. Darksant pressed the edge of his blade against Danta's throat.

Santa moved with urgency, approaching Darksant with purposeful steps. He carefully removed his hat and placed it gently on the floor. With a swift, practiced motion, he pulled out several snowballs from beneath his robe and hurled them at Darksant.

One snowball struck Darksant's face, causing him to recoil and momentarily lose his vision. The remaining snowballs burst into clouds of white smoke, enveloping Darksant in a thick, obscuring haze. The swirling smoke made it difficult for Darksant to see or react to his surroundings, creating a brief but crucial window of opportunity.

In the chaos, Santa talwar. quickly grabbed Danta by the hand, and Danta snatched the hat from the floor. Together, they sprinted back to Avnith, Aiva, and Vini. Darksant's furious roar filled the hall as he shouted, "Attack!" His kobolds surged forward at his command.

Through the swirling smoke, Vini was the first to spot the eerie sight of the Kobold army. A five-foot-tall panda and teddy bears studded with sharp bits loomed large, while toy robots with glowing red eyes added to the menace. Fashion dolls, a china doll, and rag dolls hung limply, their features frozen in unsettling expressions. Heidi Plusczok dolls and Matryoshka dolls jumped around wildly, their movements erratic. Superhero action figures posed aggressively, and puppets like Kathputli and marionettes, now without strings, moved in a disturbing manner. Military action figures, complete with tanks, helicopters, and planes, were firing at Santa and the children.

Amid this chaotic army, Chinya and Bhola stood out, their eyes gleaming with a sinister glint. The sight was overwhelming; the toys seemed endless, filling the hallway with their chilling presence as they marched menacingly toward Santa and the kids. Darksant's black smoke twisted into a bow and arrow. He aimed it at Santa and shot a dark arrow that hit Santa on the right side of hisback. Santa lurched forward from the pain, and the spruce twig fell from his hand. Moaning in pain, Santa staggered as Avnith reached out to help him up, but in his haste, accidentally tore a small piece of Santa's robe. Meanwhile, Aiva quickly grabbed the fallen twig, determined to keep it safe.

"Run!" Santa urged, his voice strained. The five of them—Avnith, Vini, Danta, Aiva, and Santa—climbed onto the platform of thirteen tunnels. One by one, the tunnel openings began to close with a resounding "STOONK!"

Before the tunnel next to Aiva could close, she dragged Santa and Danta into it, and they disappeared just as the tunnel sealed shut. Only three tunnels remained open, and Avnith and Vini were still outside.

"Fast!" Avnith shouted as he jumped into the tunnel, but just as Vini was about to follow, Chinya and Bhola's hands clamped around her legs, dragging her back.

"Help!" Vini cried, her voice filled with terror. Avnith, in a panic, tried to pull her in, but the army of action figures—soldiers, ancient warriors—opened fire with guns and arrows. Avnith groaned as several projectiles struck him, causing him to lose his grip on Vini's arm.

"Vini, no!" he shouted, but it was too late. Chinya and Bhola yanked her back into the horde, and the tunnel shut with a final, heart-wrenching "STOONK!" right in front of Avnith's face.

Panting and wounded, Avnith was left in the suffocating darkness of the tunnel, the cries of his sister still echoing in his ears.

CHAPTER 6

Menace of Unexplored Himalayas

The Deodar forest lay still under the glow of the luminous moon, its snow-covered landscape creating an enchanting yet eerie atmosphere. The forest stood silent.

Amid this wintry stillness, a sudden burst of blue light illuminated the surroundings as the portal opened a few feet above the ground. Santa tumbled out of the portal and hit the snow-covered ground with a thud, groaning in discomfort as the cold stung his body, while Aiva, still mid-fall, struggled to regain her balance. Danta emerged from the portal, tumbling unceremoniously onto the ground, his face buried in the snow.

"Someone, please help me," Danta pleaded, his voice muffled by the snow. Aiva, attempting to catch her breath, snapped back, "Stop yelling for a second."

Santa lay on the ground, his arms and legs sprawled out. "I think I've broken my back," he said, wincing in pain. Despite feeling hurt and disoriented, they were relieved to be back in the safe Deodar forest, away from the dark chamber.

In the peaceful Deodar forest, they took a break. Santa leaned against a tall tree, sipping from his flask. Aiva and

Danta were also catching their breath and recovering from their tough escape.

Aiva saw dark veins spreading up Santa's neck and felt a chill of fear. "Santa, what's happening?" she asked, her voice shaking.

Santa looked at her with a worried expression. "It's dark magic venom," he said.

Aiva's worry grew. "This looks serious."

Santa replied, trying to stay calm, "Yep. This is Darksant's magic. The venom is spreading fast. If I don't get help before sunrise, it'll be too late for me."

Aiva's eyes widened. "What do we do? How can we help?"

Santa took a painful breath, his irritation evident. "Didn't I tell you? There's an emergency button on my sleigh that sends an SOS to Santa Base. But without my sleigh, we're in trouble."

Danta, looking scared, said, " Fuck."

Aiva glared at him. "Watch your language, Danta." She turned back to Santa. "There must be something we can do. We can't let you die."

Santa, still in pain, tried to stay positive. "Don't worry! I'm tough. The good news is, my hat can slow the venom down." He turned to Danta. "Give me my hat."

Danta's eyes grew wide. "Ah! I think I left it behind during the chaos."

Santa's face turned angry. "By the beard of Saint Nicholas, Now I'm going to die!" He glared at Danta.

Santa struggled to his feet, with Aiva and Danta supporting him. Just then, a sound echoed through the forest—a rustling that made Santa freeze. "What...what was that?"

Danta, his eyes wide with fear, pointed shakily in the direction of the noise. Aiva and Santa turned to see a massive Asian black bear staring back at them.

The bear's eyes glinted in the moonlight as it took a cautious step forward. The three of them stood frozen, hearts pounding, breaths shallow.

Santa whispered urgently, "Nobody moves."

But before the words had fully left his mouth, Danta turned and bolted. Aiva, her instincts kicking in, followed him without a second thought. The bear roared, the sound reverberating through the forest, and charged after them.

"Oh, holy snowballs," Santa muttered, realising he had no choice but to run as well.

The bear charged after them, its massive paws thundering against the ground. Santa, moving with a speed that belied his bulk, quickly outpaced Aiva and Danta. The bear, however, was gaining on the children, its powerful strides closing the gap.

As the bear opened its jaws to grab them, Aiva and Danta leapt between two joined tree branches. The bear's jaws clamped shut, getting stuck in the narrow space. It pulled free with a roar of frustration and continued the chase.

Bursting out of the forest, Aiva and Danta found themselves at the edge of a cliff where Santa stood, scanning the horizon. Unable to control their momentum, they collided with Santa, and all three tumbled over the edge. Luckily, the snow cushioned their fall, and they rolled down the slope until they came to a stop at the base of a rocky hill.

Breathless and bruised, they found themselves cornered in a dead end, surrounded by steep, jagged walls. The bear began its slow descent toward them, its menacing growls echoing through the narrow space. Each step brought it closer, its eyes locked on them.

"Damn it, Santa, do something!" Danta shouted, panic evident in his voice. "You're Santa Claus. You must have superpowers!"

Aiva pulled out the spruce twig, hoping it would transform into a talwar, but it did not change.

She handed the spruce twig to Santa, but as he tried to lift it, his arm fell limply. The tiny twig seemed too heavy for him. A piercing scream echoed in Santa's ears as he groaned in pain. "I can't use the talwar," he said through gritted teeth. "Darksant's venom is draining my strength, making it impossible to weild the talwar."

Danta, scared, asked, "What nonsense is that?"

Santa shot Danta a stern look. Aiva picked up the spruce twig, trying desperately to transform it into a talwar. She focused hard, but nothing happened.

Santa urged calmly, "Focus, Aiva."

The bear was getting closer, its growls growing louder with each step. Santa's calm began to waver as he grew more nervous. "Hurry, Aiva!" he and Danta shouted in unison, their voices rising in panic as the bear loomed ever nearer.

Aiva struggled to change the twig into a talwar. "I'm trying! Stop yelling at me!"

The bear roared loudly, almost on top of them. Santa, thinking quickly, suddenly remembered something. "Roar," he muttered. "Of course!"

Reaching into his magic pocket, Santa pulled out his flask of shimmering green liquid and gulped it down. As the bear lunged, Aiva and Danta screamed. Santa pounded his chest, and his body inflated like a balloon. His mouth stretched wide open, and he let out an earth-shattering roar. The sound waves blasted the bear, sending it flying backward to the top of the cliff. Snow swirled violently, whipped into a frenzy by the force of the roar. Aiva and Danta covered their ears, eyes wide in astonishment.

As the roar subsided, the snow settled, and the bear scrambled to its feet, whimpering. It turned and fled into the forest.

Danta's face lit up with relief. "You did it!" he said, hugging Santa.

Santa, smiling weakly and breathing heavily, looked uncomfortable with the hug. Blood speckled his lips as he coughed. He glanced at his skin through the torn piece of his right shoulder robe, which had been ripped by Avnith in

Darksant's tower. His skin was dark and decayed, showing the visible marks of Darksant's venom.

Aiva, disappointed that she couldn't transform the spruce twig into a talwar, carefully placed it back into Santa's magical pocket.

"I hope Avnith and Vini are safe," Aiva said, her voice filled with worry.

Santa and Danta exchanged anxious glances.

Meanwhile, high in the serene Himalayan wilderness, the large Himalayan owl sat quietly on a pine tree, hooting softly under the bright full moon.

The moonlight bathed the landscape in a magical glow, illuminating the expansive pine forests, snow-covered peaks, and tranquil hills.

In the distance, a frozen pond glistened like clear glass under the moonlight. Suddenly, a bright blue light began to glow beneath the ice, casting an enchanting aura over the pond's surface.

Beneath the shimmering ice, a portal briefly opened and expelled Avnith before closing and vanishing into nothingness. Avnith found himself trapped underwater, his face etched with panic. He pounded desperately on the thick ice above him, but it remained unyielding. His screams were muffled by the cold, dark water, with only a stream of bubbles rising slowly toward the surface. The freezing temperature bit into his skin, and the frigid water drained his strength with each passing second.

Desperately, he swam to the edge of the pond, his eyes scanning for any thin patches of ice. Just as his vision started to blur and his consciousness began to fade, he spotted a faint crack in the ice..

He pounded on the thin layer of ice, feeling it yield slightly beneath his fists. The cold water was unbearable, and his vision was growing dim. On the brink of drowning, with the frigid embrace of the pond threatening to pull him into oblivion, Avnith summoned every ounce of his remaining strength and made one final, desperate attempt.

The ice cracked. With a surge of adrenaline, he broke through, clawing at the opening as he pulled himself up. He crawled onto the frozen surface, his breaths coming in rapid, shallow gasps. His body shook uncontrollably from the cold as he dragged himself away from the pond, his wet clothes freezing against his skin.

He collapsed onto the snowy ground, lying on his back, panting heavily. His chest heaved as he tried to catch his breath, his eyes wide with shock and exhaustion. Above him, the starry night sky stretched infinitely, a stark contrast to the life-threatening ordeal he had just endured.

Avnith lay on the snowy ground, shivering from the cold. His breaths came out in ragged puffs, forming clouds in the freezing air. Just as he started to calm down, he heard a low, menacing growl.

Turning his head slowly, Avnith's eyes widened in fear. A pack of Himalayan wolves stood at the edge of the pine forest, their eyes glowing with hunger. The wolves' growls grew louderas they focused on Avnith. They were ready to attack.

Panic surged through him, giving him a burst of energy. He scrambled to his feet and ran, his legs propelling him across the frozen pond. The wolves gave chase, their powerful legs closing the distance quickly. With each desperate step Avnith took, the ice beneath him began to crack, spider-webbing outwards, threatening to give way at any moment.

He nearly slipped, his feet struggling to find purchase on the slick surface, but he managed to stay upright, narrowly avoiding another plunge into the icy depths. The alpha wolf, larger and more fearsome than the rest, barked an order. One of the wolves lunged at Avnith, but its leap carried it straight into a newly formed hole in the ice, sending it plunging into the freezing water below.

Avnith was exhausted and freezing. His legs felt as heavy as lead. He stumbled, and the alpha wolf's claws slashed his leg, causing him to fall onto the ice. He slid across the surface and stopped, with the wolves circling around him, growling and staring hungrily.

His vision darkened, and his strength waned. He saw the alpha wolf crouch, ready to attack. Everything seemed to slow down, and he felt doomed. Suddenly, a mysterious figure leaped over him and stood between him and the alpha wolf. As the wolf pounced on the figure, the figure swung a war hammer with a swift motion. The alpha wolf let out a whimper as it slid across the ice, its menace subdued. Through his blurry vision, Avnith saw a mysterious figure leaping over him. The figure roared fiercely, and the alpha wolf, now hurt, got up and fled, followed by the other wolves. Avnith's vision went completely darkashis body succumbed to exhaustion and cold. He heard the wolves' retreating howls and felt the presence of his unknown rescuer before everything went black.

Meanwhile, far from the icy pond, an old spyglass telescope jutted out from a rocky cliff like a giant periscope. This was no ordinary telescope—it was the "Doordarshan Doorbin," or "DD" for short. Its long, snake-like structure stretched from the cliff's edge down to where Aiva stood, her eye pressed to the lens. The ancient mechanisms whirred as Aiva peered through, scanning the distant landscape for any sign of danger or help. The world through the "DD" lens appeared sharper and more vivid, revealing details far beyond normal sight.

Aiva, wrapped in a long faux fur coat, looked intently through the DD, trying to figure out where they were. Next to her, Danta, wearing a furry ear flap hat, watched with interest. "I want to see too!" he said, reaching for the DD.

"This isn't the time to play around, Danta," Aiva snapped, her voice edged with urgency. She squinted through the lens, her breath misting in the cold air. "I found it!" she exclaimed, excitement and relief mingling in her voice.

Santa, wearing earmuffs, joined Aiva. She stepped aside to let Santa look through the DD..

Santa peered through the lens of the DD, his eyes narrowing as the view sharpened on the distant peak. For the first time, he saw Darksant's tower. The structure loomed ominously, casting a dark shadow over the snowy expanse. Massive, dark tentacles coiled around the ancient stone, swaying with a disturbing, almost sentient motion. The sight sent a shiver down Santa's spine. Santa closed the DD, which coiled back into its resting position like a snake. Danta pouted, "I wanted to see too."

Santa scolded him with a cough, "No need. I know about you. You're on the naughty list. Because of you, everyone is in trouble."

Danta replied, "But you said it was because of Avnith Bhaiya."

Santa said, "Yes, both of you. Pain in the Brass."

Danta looked sad. Aiva comforted him, trying to make him feel better.

Santa coughed again, a deeper, more concerning sound. "Wish I had my sleigh. The CPD would be here by now."

Aiva's curiosity got the better of her. "CPD? What's that?"

Santa smiled faintly, shaking his head. "Christmas Police Department. Don't ask more; I won't tell."

The children looked at each other, confused.

Aiva asked, "Santa, how can we climb this rocky mountain and snowy cliff? We're stuck here."

Santa sat down on the ground, looking defeated. "We can't," he said.

He fell silent, trying to think of what to do next.

Meanwhile, far from the desolate peak, there was a small, oval-shaped room made of Deodar wood, with a low ceiling that required anyone to stoop. Wooden blocks supported the cozy structure. The compact space made the kitchen easily visible. An old kettle sat on the stove, gently steaming with smoke curling from its spout. A winding staircase led to the upper floor. Various herbs and kitchen tools hung from the ceiling. Candles scattered around the room cast a warm, festive glow, adding to the inviting atmosphere.

Avnith woke up, wrapped snugly in a blanket, and sat in a wooden chair next to a crackling fire. He glanced down at his clothes—they were dry and warm, as if he had never been submerged in the freezing pond. Shocked and disoriented, he tried to process the sudden change in his circumstances.

His thoughts were interrupted by the sound of loud footsteps approaching. He let out a startled scream as a dwarf-elf appeared. The dwarf-elf was striking in appearance: he was short and sturdy, his pointed ears jutting out from beneath a mop of silver hair. He wore clothes crafted from the fur of a snow bear, the thick, white pelts stitched together in an intricate pattern that shimmered faintly in the firelight. His massive beard, braided and adorned with small silver bells, reached down to his chest, giving him a wise and imposing look. An eye patch covered his right eye, adding an air of mystery and ruggedness to his weathered face.

He carried a heavy tankard, its metal gleaming in the firelight. With a gruff yet kindly tone, he handed it to Avnith and said, "Drink this."

Avnith hesitantly took the tankard, peering nervously at the thick green fluid inside. The dwarf-elf's stern gaze bore into him, leaving Avnith no choice but to comply. He forced a swallow, grimacing at the taste. "What was that?" he asked, his voice trembling.

"It's poison," the dwarf-elf replied, his expression unchanging.

Avnith's heart raced with fear. The dwarf-elf then pulled out a torn piece of Santa's robe and demanded, "Tell me, kid, where did you find this?"

"S-Santa Claus," Avnith stammered.

"Which country?" the dwarf-elf pressed.

"India," Avnith replied, his voice shaking.

The dwarf-elf's face fell in disappointment. "Don't tell me it's Santosh Chaube."

Avnith, still reeling from the revelation that he had ingested poison, nodded frantically. "Please, save me," he pleaded.

The dwarf-elf's frustration erupted like a storm as he slammed his fist on the table next to him, causing Avnith to flinch in fear.

"What happened to the Arctic Circle Santa Selection Board?" He bellowed, his voice echoing off the wooden walls. "They start hiring anyone these days. I thought Santas from the US or UK or Russian would come, but here we have an Indian Santa Claus!" He crushed the tankard in his hand.

Avnith, trembling, pleaded for help. "Please, help me. I'm poisoned."

The dwarf-elf's demeanour softened slightly as he examined Avnith. "Relax, kid," he said gruffly. "It's not poison. It's a potion to boost your energy." Avnith felt a wave of relief wash over him as the tension in the room eased.

Tollbo took a seat next to Avnith and gently touched his clothes to check if they were fully dry. "Hmm," he murmured, satisfied. "The ancient flames worked properly."

"Do you know Santosh Chaube?" Avnith asked cautiously.

Tollbosighed deeply. "Unfortunately, yes. He was one of the naughtiest cadets I've ever seen at the Arctic Circle Santa Selection Board."

"But who are you?" Avnith pressed, curiosity overcoming his fear.

"I'm Tollbo Bolbole, General of the Dwarf-Elf Army in Arctic Warfare," Tollbo replied proudly.

Avnith's eyes widened in curiosity. "How did you find me?"

Tollbo Bolbole produced a compass from his pocket, its dial spinning gently as if guided by an unseen force. "This is the Compass of Seekers," Tollbo explained. "Invented by the one and only Saint Nicholas himself. It leads me to those I seek. I sensed Santa nearby and was heading toward him, but I stumbled upon you instead."

Avnith marvelled at the magic of the compass, its intricate markings and glowing needle holding an otherworldly allure. "Do you know Darksant?" Avnith asked tentatively.

Tollbo Bolbole's eyes filled with anger. "I know him better than anyone. I wish this compass worked on him. If it did, Darksant would be dead by now."

Avnith swallowed hard, understanding the seriousness of Tollbo Bolbole's words.

Meanwhile, in the dark and foreboding chamber of Darksant, the atmosphere was thick with malevolence. Darksant sat on his imposing throne, a dark aura surrounding him. Beside him, Vini was confined in a birdcage hanging from the ceiling. Despite the grim situation, she looked calm and unfazed.

"You're the bad guy," Vini said bravely. "You should stop this and try to be a good person."

Darksant laughed loudly, his voice dripping with malice. "Good? I don't care about being good," he sneered.

Vini countered, "Good people have happy endings."

Darksant's scornful laugh echoed through the chamber. "Happy endings are for those who believe in fairy tales," he said dismissively.

Vini stared at Darksant, her eyes filled with a mixture of defiance and determination. "My mother always said that bad guys never find happiness in the end."

Darksant's grin widened, his eyes gleaming with malevolence. "Your mother was right," he said, his voice dripping with dark amusement. "Bad guys never find happiness in the end because we don't seek it. We seek power."

With a sudden, fluid motion, Darksant enveloped himself in a swirling mass of dark smoke. From his back, sinister tentacles began to emerge, their dark forms undulating and writhing. They helped him rise gracefully toward Vini's cage, their malevolent presence casting eerie shadows on the walls. The tentacles reached out, wrapping around the bars of Vini's cage with a crushing force.

Vini gasped in horror as the metal creaked and bent under the relentless pressure. Her eyes widened in terror as the bars started to constrict around her, and she cried out, "Ahhh! You're bad! Santa is good. He'll come for you!" Darksant's eyes gleamed with twisted delight as he watched her struggle. His evil grin widened, savoring her fear and anguish as the cage continued to creak."I'm waiting," Darksant hissed, his voice a chilling whisper in the darkness. He gripped the bars of the cage with his tentacled fingers, curling them around with eerie strength. "I'm waiting for the good guys to come. They'll have to come." As Darksant spoke, dark tentacles began to envelope the birdcage completely. Vini's fear overwhelmed her, and she started to cry as the shadows closed in around her.

CHAPTER 7

Ode to the Fall of Indian Christmas

Note to Readers: Italicised text in this chapter indicates flashback scenes. These sections provide background and context, offering insights into the characters' pasts.

Santa's once vibrant and robust figure was now weakened, with the darkness of Darksant's magic spreading like a sinister shadow across the lower part of his body. It crawled ominously up his chest and arm, darkening his skin and sapping his strength with each passing moment. Aiva and Danta were desperately trying to figure out how to escape their predicament. The towering rocky mountain was unclimbable.

Santa looked out at the horizon with a heavy heart. "The sun will rise soon," he said quietly. He turned to Aiva and Danta, his eyes showing deep sadness. "I haven't delivered any gifts yet. If I don't do it before sunrise..."

Danta interrupted, "You lose your job, they won't pay you, and they'll put you in jail. You've told us that a thousand times."

Santa's voice shook. "No. If I don't deliver the gifts before sunrise, Indian children will lose their belief in Christmas... AGAIN, and it will be lost forever."

Aiva and Danta were shocked, understanding how serious it was. Aiva asked, "Santa, what do you mean by AGAIN? Who is this Darksant?"

Santa took a deep breath, looking tired. "Darksant is the personification of all the negativity and doubt about Christmas. Every time someone doubts the holiday spirit or stops believing in the magic of this season, Darksant becomes stronger."

Santa began to recount the tale, his voice carrying the weight of history as Aiva and Danta listened intently. "Long ago," he started, "Christmas was celebrated in India much like any other country. Back then, the traditional green outfit worn by Santa Claus was a symbol of nature and the changing season's spirit, a tradition that persisted until the intrusion of Coca-Cola, which influenced a change in our costume. Bloody, Santa Association Boards."

He paused, his eyes reflecting the pain of the past. "Darksant's real name, before he was consumed by darkness, was Darpin Darka. He was India's first Santa Claus."

Santa's voice grew sombre as he continued, "Darpin wanted to deliver more gifts. But in India, fewer children believed in Christmas compared to other places. He longed to reach more children and spread more happiness across the globe. In his desperation, he pleaded with St. Nicholas to extend his reach. But St. Nicholas, fearful of the potential consequences, denied his request. He worried that Darpin's deep love for spreading joy might lead him to madness."

Santa paused, his gaze distant as he recalled the past. "Unfortunately, St. Nicholas's fears became a reality. Frustrated and disheartened, Darpin began to interfere with the duties of other Santas. His desire to spread joy turned into a desperate obsession."

"St. Nicholas was furious," Santa explained, his voice thick with the memory. "He told Darpin that if he continued to defy orders, he'd lose everything—his job, his freedom. But Darpin, humiliated and consumed by rage, refused to listen. His pride wouldn't let him bend."

Santa paused, his expression clouded with sorrow and regret. "In the end, St. Nicholas had no choice but to order Darpin's imprisonment. It wasn't out of malice... but to protect Christmas and the magic we were meant to safeguard. That's when everything changed. The darkness took hold."

The Dwarf-Elf army had captured Darpin, their most dangerous adversary, and locked him in a cage-like coffin. Cold iron bars, thick and unyielding, pressed in on him. As the army marched him aboard their colossal ship bound for the Arctic, the winds howled as though nature itself sensed the dark fate awaiting him.

The Dwarf-Elf fleet was a sight to behold: massive ships of ancient craftsmanship built from enchanted timber reinforced with iron and gold. Their hulls, designed to endure the wrath of the sea, glistened with carved designs of fierce creatures and runes. These were no ordinary vessels—they were battle-hardened, enchanted to withstand the deadliest of voyages. Their sharp prows sliced through the frozen sea, cutting through thick layers of ice with brutal efficiency as if cleaving the bones of an ancient, slumbering giant.

Amidst the frozen, desolate waters, the army gathered in silence at the ship's edge. Their breath fogged the air, mingling with the icy mist. With solemn resolve, they tipped the coffin forward, sending it plunging into the icy depths below. The water swallowed it whole, the iron creaking under the weight of the frozen abyss.

As the coffin sank, the dark sea seemed to claim Darpin for itself, pulling him into an unforgiving grave beneath the ice. The last echoes of the iron cage faded into the deep, the army watching in silence, hoping this would be the end of him—for good.

The coffin sank deeper into the abyss, the faint glimmers of light from above fading into all-consuming darkness as the icy water pressed in from all sides. Inside the iron prison, Darpin's breath grew shallow, his chest rising and falling with the weight of his impending doom. The biting cold seeped through his bones, and his vision dimmed as he accepted his fate. His eyes, once sharp and full of defiance, now closed tightly as he let the black void envelop him.

But the abyss had other plans.

From the depths of the murky water, dark, writhing tentacle-like creatures emerged, slithering around the coffin with unsettling speed, almost hypnotic as they circled the iron bars, drawn to Darpin's still form within. The creatures, ancient and unnatural, twisted and coiled, their slick forms undulating like predators that had waited eons for this moment.

In a sickening display of unity, the tentacles slithered into the coffin, slipping through the gaps to seek out Darpin's motionless body. Without hesitation, they forced their way into his nostrils, ears, and mouth, merging with him in a grotesque and unnatural fusion. His body jerked violently as the creatures pulsed through his veins, dark energy fusing with his very soul, twisting and distorting it.

The darkness was not his end—it was his rebirth.

Santa's voice trembled as he recounted the horror. "The darkness embraced him. The tentacled creatures invaded his very being, resurrecting him with a horrific new purpose."

Darpin's eyes snapped open, wild with terror and rage. His chest heaved, and he let out a guttural scream that echoed through the dark waters. As the sound tore from his throat, a small, writhing tentacle forced its way out of his mouth, shaking uncontrollably as it dangled in the freezing air. His body convulsed violently, possessed by the dark forces now coursing through his veins.

The creatures had claimed him. His soul, once his own, was now bound to a sinister mission beyond his control. The tentacle slithered back inside as Darpin's scream faded, but the darkness within him remained.

Santa's tone grew darker as he spoke. "The darkness gave him new orders—a new purpose: to destroy Christmas and St. Nicholas. And so, Darpin, now twisted into the monstrous Darksant, began his relentless quest to undo the very magic he once cherished."

He paused, his voice heavy with sorrow. "Darksant began manipulating all the Santas, convincing them that they were mere puppets of St. Nicholas," Santa continued, bitterness lacing his words. "While they labored tirelessly to spread joy and hope, Darksant claimed that St. Nicholas remained aloof, comfortable in his palace, untouched by the struggles of the world."

Santa's voice trembled as he recounted the final part of the story. "In the end, St. Nicholas had no choice—he sentenced Darksant to death to save Christmas. But Darksant... he was too powerful, too consumed by rage. He returned from the darkness more vengeful than ever."

Santa's face grew pale. "Darksant slaughtered every reindeer, every Santa Claus who stood in his way. No one was spared, especially the Indian Santa Claus. The horror of what happened spread quickly—no one wanted to be the next Indian Santa Claus. They were terrified of Darksant. The gifts stopped coming, and the children in India, who once believed so deeply, began to lose hope. That's when the dark age of Christmas began."

Santa's eyes shimmered with unshed tears as he looked at Aiva and Danta. The weight of the past seemed to bear down on him, his shoulders sagging under the burden of lost hope. "Since that day," he said softly, "India stopped celebrating Christmas. The joy and magic of the season vanished, leaving only emptiness."

He took a deep breath, the sorrow in his eyes hardening into fierce determination. "This is why it's crucial that we stop Darksant," he declared. "Weneed to restore Christmas and protect the belief of those who still hold it dear. If we don't, the darkness will win, and the magic of Christmas will be lost forever."

Aiva, her curiosity piqued, asked, "But if Darksant was so powerful, how did St. Nicholas manage to save Christmas back then? And how are we still celebrating Christmas today?"

Santa took a deep breath, the weight of past memories pressingheavily on him. "Because St. Nicholas commanded a war against Darksant."

Danta, just as curious, leaned in closer. "Who fought for St. Nicholas? Warriors? Ninjas?"

Santa's eyes gleamed with a blend of pride and sorrow. "Dwarf-Elves," he said softly. "They were the bravest and most loyal soldiers of St. Nicholas."

Meanwhile, in Tollbo's cosy, compact house, Avnith and Tollbo sat in front of a crackling fireplace. Avnith held a tankard of the greenish potion Tollbo had given him, while Tollbo puffed on his pipe, the smoke curling lazily toward the low ceiling.

"Then what happened?" Avnith asked, his voice barely a whisper, captivated by the story.

Tollbo gazed into the dancing flames for a moment before beginning his tale. "St. Nicholas prepared an army of Dwarf-Elves," he explained, his voice rich with nostalgia. "You see, Dwarf-Elves never lost any battle."

As Tollbo spoke, the memory came alive in his mind. "St. Nicholas used his magical powers to create the magnificent Haladie, a double-edged dagger known as Vojas. Only this dagger could kill Darksant and save Indian Christmas. He handed it to our General, Nimrol Nolro."

On a snowy battlefield nestled deep in the Himalayas, a war of unspeakable fury raged. The once-pristine snow was now churned into a slush of crimson as Darksant's black, writhing tentacles swept across the landscape like shadows of death. His dark, inhuman appendages moved with terrifying speed and power, cutting down half of the Dwarf-Elf army with ruthless efficiency.

Among the fallen was Nimrol. He lay motionless, his eyes open but devoid of life, surrounded by the bodies of his comrades. The legendary Vojas dagger lay inches from his lifeless hand, glinting faintly in the pale, cold light of the snowy wasteland. The weapon, a symbol of hope and strength, seemed almost forlorn in the brutal scene, its once-proud gleam now diminished by the blood-soaked ground.

But the surviving Dwarf-Elves did not falter. With a roar that echoed through the freezing air, they charged at Darksant. Their small but sturdy bodies, clothed in battle-worn armour, moved with precision and courage. Each step was filled with defiance, their spirits undaunted despite the devastation unfolding around them. They wielded swords, axes, and war hammers, striking at the dark tentacles that thrashed through the air, trying to fend off the relentless evil.

Darksant, towering above them, watched with malevolent delight. His tentacles lashed out, crushing anything in their path, but the Dwarf-Elves kept coming. The snow beneath their feet was soaked in blood, but their resolve was unshaken. They fought not only for their lives but for the very soul of Christmas itself.

The battlefield was a spectacle of destruction. Huge fissures in the ground opened where Darksant's dark magic pulsed while the air was filled with the sounds of clashing weapons, the screams of the wounded, and the eerie hiss of the tentacles as they tore through flesh and bone. Yet, amidst this chaos, the Dwarf-Elves fought on. They were outnumbered and outmatched, but their will was unbreakable. The snowstorm intensified, swirling around them as if the very elements were mourning the brave lives lost and the battle still raging.

Darksant, in a desperate bid to end the battle once and for all, unleashed the full force of his black, writhing tentacles upon the Dwarf-Elf army. The battlefield became a swirling maelstrom of dark smoke, thick and suffocating, obscuring all sight. The once fierce and proud Dwarf-Elves, who had fought valiantly despite their losses, were now enveloped in the oppressive darkness. The sound of steel clashing against unnatural limbs faded into silence, leaving only the haunting whistle of the wind as it cut through the smoke.

When the dark fog finally settled, the battlefield revealed a scene of utter devastation. Darksant stood alone amidst the carnage, his chest heaving with laboured breaths, weak but filled with a twisted sense of pride. His once-mighty black tentacles, now slack and depleted, drooped limply at his sides. Around him lay the bodies of the fallen, their once-determined faces now cold and lifeless in the snow. The proud army of the Dwarf-Elves had been decimated, a grim testament to Darksant's wrath and relentless power.

But as Darksant surveyed the destruction with cruel satisfaction, movement caught his eye.

There, amid the sea of bodies and broken weapons, stood one figure—Tollbo, the last warrior of the Dwarf-Elf army.

Unlike the others, he had survived the onslaught, his stance steady despite the overwhelming loss that surrounded him. His eyes, sharp and unyielding, glinted with a mixture of defiance and deep sorrow.

Tollbo faced Darksant, his posture unwavering, his heart heavy with the weight of those who had fallen. There was no fear in his gaze, only a fierce resolve that had been forged in the fires of battle and the depths of loss. He was the last of his kind on this field, the final hope for avenging his comrades and the spirit of Christmas that had been so cruelly tarnished.

Darksant, though weakened, straightened and sneered at the lone warrior, his voice a low growl. "You are the last. Just one Dwarf-Elf. Do you think you can stand against me?"

Tollbo remained silent, his grip tightening on the hilt of his war hammer. The weapon felt heavier now, but there was no turning back.

With a roar that echoed through the frozen air, Tollbo charged at Darksant; his war hammer raised high, the snow beneath his feet parting as he launched himself into the final, fateful battle.

Tollbo's eyes glinted with the memory of the duel. "We fought like mad," he said, his voice cutting through the intense recollection. His words were heavy with the weight of the past, each syllable a reminder of the chaos and bravery that had marked that fateful day.

Tollbo's expression hardened as he continued, "Every swing of my war hammer, every clash of steel, was a desperate attempt to turn the tide. But the darkness... it was relentless."

In the heart of the battlefield, Darksant's black longsword swung through the air with deadly grace, its edge gleaming with malevolent intent. Each swing of the blade was a testament to his dark power, slicing effortlessly through the frigid air. With a sudden, ruthless motion, he delivered a brutal gash across Tollbo's right eye. The blade sliced through flesh and bone, leaving a deep, gaping wound. Blood erupted from the cut in a visceral spray, staining Tollbo's face and armour.

The pain was immediate and searing, a white-hot agony that forced Tollbo to his knees. He clutched his face with a hoarse gasp, the intense hurt making his breaths come in ragged, painful bursts.

Darksant, towering above him, cast a long, foreboding shadow. His presence was an oppressive weight, a dark spectre looming menacingly over Tollbo. With a deliberate, measured motion, he raised his longsword high. The blade hovered above Tollbo, poised to deliver the final, crushing blow.

"I almost lost the battle," Tollbo admitted, his voice laced with the peril he had faced.

Before Darksant could bring his longsword down upon Tollbo, the last of the Dwarf-Elf warrior's resolve ignited with a fierce, desperate energy. Summoning every ounce of strength left in his battered body, Tollbo clutched the Vojas tightly. With a final, determined surge, he drove the dagger deep into Darksant's heart.

The dark sorcerer's reaction was immediate and violent. A guttural howl of excruciating pain erupted from Darksant, his eyes wide with shock and fury. His black magic tentacles, previously so menacing, writhed and flailed uncontrollably, their dark energy reacting violently to the searing wound.

In the midst of his agony, a mysterious, bright, white-blue force began to swirl around Darksant. The force intensified, its radiant glow casting eerie shadows across the battlefield. It wrapped around Darksant, lifting him off the ground and pulling him upward. The sorcerer's cries of anguish grew louder as the force dragged him back toward the craggy peak of his ominous tower.

Tollbo, weakened and drenched in his own blood, watched the spectacle unfold with a complex mix of relief and sorrow. His strength was waning, and the battlefield around him seemed to blur, but the sight of Darksant being pulled away marked a significant, bittersweet victory.

"Since that day," Tollbo explained, his voice heavy with the burden of memory and fatigue, "Darksant has been trapped in his tower, cursed to remain there and unable to leave."

Avnith listened, wide-eyed, as the gravity of the tale sank in. The room fell silent, except for the crackling of the fire, as the weight of the story lingered in the air.

Avnith gazed at Tollbo. "But you have the Vojas, right?" he asked eagerly. "We can defeat him now."

Tollbo's expression darkened, and frustration crossed his face. "I don't have it," he replied. "When Darksant was sucked back into the tower, his tentacles shattered the Vojas into two pieces. The force was so immense that the fragments were sent flying in different directions." Tollbo took a deep breath. "I searched every corner of the Himalayas, but despite my best efforts, I couldn't find them."

Avnith's voice was tinged with concern. "Is that why you didn't return home?"

Tollbo paused, his face shadowed with worry. "Yes" he said slowly. "I fear that Darksant will try to escape from the tower to reclaim the Vojas and use it against St. Nicholas."

He sighed deeply, his eyes reflecting profound fear. "The Vojas was meant to kill Darksant, not just trap him in the tower. His darkness is powerful, and I know he will use every trick he has to escape and endanger Christmas once more. Someone has to stay here to guard Christmas from him."

Avnith nodded, absorbing the gravity of Tollbo's words. "He played his trick. Darksant has Santa's sleigh. But why does he need Santa's hat and robe?"

Tollbo's face tightened with the seriousness of the moment as he prepared to explain.

Meanwhile, in the crisp, cold air of the Himalayan wilderness, Santa, Aiva, and Danta huddled together, their breath misting in the icy night. Aiva, her voice trembling yet resolute, turned to Santa and asked the same question that lingered in Avnith's mind. "Why does Darksant need your robe and hat?"

Santa, still weak but with his eyes blazing with resolve, took a deep breath. "The Santa Claus hat and robe hold many powers," he began, his voice steady despite the cold.

"Darksant already has my sleigh, which he needs to escape. However, to leave his tower, he also needs my robe and hat."

Aiva's eyes widened in realisation. "So, it's not just about escaping; he needs them to survive."

Santa nodded solemnly. "Exactly. The St. Nicholas curse binds him to his tower. Only the magic of the Santa hat and robe can shield him from it. Without these, Darksant would die the moment he tried to leave."

Aiva's brow furrowed with concern. "We have to stop him." She rose to her feet like a warrior, her eyes blazing with determination. "Let's save Christmas."

"Danta gasped, his face a mix of exhaustion and uncertainty. He looked at Santa, then at Aiva, and with a weary sigh added, 'I just want to go home. So, let's save Christmas and get this over with.' Despite his tiredness and doubt, his resolve to help shone through."

Santa, feeling a surge of energy from their determination and bravery, nodded. Just as he opened his mouth to speak, the air around them seemed to ripple with eerie energy. Out of nowhere, kobolds—cute, big-eyed stuffed monkey dolls—sprang from the shadows. They lunged at Aiva and Danta, knocking them to the ground with a hard thud.

Santa turned to help, but before he could react, a small, elderly gnome doll landed before him. The gnome doll, holding a bright purple ball, whispered, "Zu Darksant," and hurled it toward Santa. A portal, shimmering with purple light, opened instantly and sucked Santa into it before he could resist. The portal closed with a snap, leaving Aiva and Danta screaming, "Santa!"

The stuffed monkey dolls quickly tied up Aiva and Danta, lifting them off the ground effortlessly. The gnome doll, with an air of grim efficiency, produced another purple ball. Whispering once again, "Zu Darksant," hethrew it at the struggling children. A new portal swirled open, its edges crackling with magical energy.

Aiva and Danta were pulled into the vortex, their cries for Santa fading as the portal absorbed them. The stuffed monkey dolls, now animated and jittery, danced chaotically, leaping into the vortex one by one. The gnome doll leapt into the portal after them, and the portal disappeared as suddenly as it had appeared. The clearing was left silent and empty.

Meanwhile, Tollbo, suited up in his armour, meticulously rummaged through a large wooden trunk filled with mystical items.

The trunk was a treasure trove of magical artefacts, each item more captivating than the last. Among the contents were intricately carved wands. A few glass jars contained swirling, captured elements: thunderbolts crackling within their confines, cyclones whirling with a soft, menacing hum, and a snowstorm, its frosty tendrils swirling in an eternal dance.

Beside the jars lay a pair of boots, their soles adorned with an ethereal cloud-like pattern, hinting at their power to carry the wearer across great distances with the mere thought of flight. Ancient-looking armour, its chest intricately engraved with sun symbols, was folded carefully in one corner.

At the centre of the collection was a Roopchoga, a magical cloak of stunning craftsmanship. When worn, this cloak granted the wearer the ability to transform into any object desired, blending seamlessly into the surroundings or assuming a completely different form. Scattered around were small boxes of bluish chalk, their contents glowing faintly with a shimmering light.

Avnith watched intently, his eyes wide with fascination as he observed the magical relics. His gaze was drawn to a small pouch from which a faint blue light emanated.

Tollbo finally grabbed the compass. With a determined snap, he shut the trunk and turned to Avnith.

Avnith, his curiosity overcoming his hesitation, asked, "How are you so sure Santa, Danta, and Aiva will be at Darksant's tower right now?"

"The sun will be up in less than two hours," he murmured. "The sleigh is still with Darksant. If Santosh wants to save Christmas, he needs his sleigh. And Darksant won't miss this golden opportunity to break his curse. He needs the hat and robe before sunrise. So either Santa, and your brother, and friends go to Darksant, or Darksant sends his kobolds to them... Eventually, they will all end up at his tower."

"But you said the compass doesn't work on Darksant," Avnith pointed out. "How will you find his tower? It was cursed, right?"

Tollbo smiled, a glint of hope in his eyes. "Vini is a pure believer. And it is said that when a true believer enters Darksant's tower of their own free will, without any force, the curse will be broken. Anyone can enter his tower, but Darksant cannot leave without the robe and hat." With that, Tollbo grabbed his war hammer and left the house.

Tollbo stepped outside into the serene snowfall. His house, a grand igloo shaped like an enormous kettle, stood proudly on the edge of a deep cliff. The igloo's exterior, crafted from large, carefully placed ice blocks, glowed faintly in the twilight, while wooden beams reinforced the structure, adding a touch of rustic charm. Smoke lazily spiraled from the spout-like chimney at the top, signaling warmth and life within. The surrounding pine forest was blanketed in snow.

Avnith, feeling a surge of responsibility and courage, pleaded, "Let me come with you."

Tollbo gave a loud whistle, summoning someone. He turned to Avnith, his face grave. "I lost 499 brothers in the war. Darksant might be weakened, but he is not powerless. Santosh and you kids have already stirred up a mess. Now it's time to finish it."

Snowflakes drifted down and settled on his broad shoulders.

From the forest emerged a fast-moving silhouette, cutting through the falling snow with remarkable speed. It skidded to a halt in front of Tollbo, dust and snow swirling around its powerful legs. As the dust settled, Avnith saw the creature clearly: a Himalayan Tahr, a majestic wild goat with a robust frame and sweeping curved horns.

Tollbo gave the Tahr a gentle pat, a fond smile spreading across his face. "Teji, my friend," he said warmly as he expertly mounted the creature's back. He turned to Avnith, his eyes serious. "Stay inside. There are more dangerous creatures in these parts than wolves. You're a smart kid—don't make foolish choices."

With that, Tollbo urged Teji forward, the Tahr's hooves thundering against the snowy ground. As he rode away, he raised his voice in a battle cry. "Come on, Teji, let's give Darksant hell!" The sound of Tollbo's call echoed through the snowy landscape, fading into the distance as he charged toward the looming threat.

Avnith stood alone, the distant growls of unseen creatures echoing through the forest. Fear gripped him, and he quickly retreated back into the safety of the igloo.

CHAPTER 8

The Christmas Climax

Note to Readers: Italicised text in this chapter indicates flashback scenes. These sections provide background and context, offering insights into the characters' pasts.

Santa's hands were ensnared in Darksant's writhing tentacles, his knees just inches above the cold, unforgiving stone floor. The malevolent figure of Darksant sat smugly on his dark throne, his grin dripping with malice. At his feet, Aiva and Danta lay bound, their faces pale with fear.

Santa's once-vibrant red suit was now drenched in the inky black venom that seeped into his skin, decaying it into a dark, twisted texture. Only his face remained untouched by the venom, but it was clear that time was running out. Soon, perhaps in an hour or less, the venom would consume him entirely, swallowing him into its dark embrace.

Though his strength was fading, Santa's voice cut through the tension with unyielding defiance. "I will not hand over my robe," he growled, staring Darksant down with fiery resolve, even as death loomed closer.

Darksant chuckled with a cold, eerie sound that echoed through the dark chamber. "I knew you would say that," he sneered. With a flick of his wrist, black smoke coiled and twisted in the air, solidifying into a long, sharp nail.

Without a moment's hesitation, Darksant drove the nail into Aiva and Danta's feet. Their piercing screams filled the chamber, echoing off the stone walls.

Vini, trapped in her cage, screamed and cried, her voice filled with terror. Santa, watching in horror, shouted, "NO!" as his heart broke for his friends. The chamber filled with the sounds of pain and despair.

Darksant's voice was cold, with no hint of mercy. "Let's not play games," he hissed. With a swift motion, his dark tentacles vanished, and Santa fell heavily to the floor, groaning in pain.

Reluctantly, Santa began to remove his red robe, his hands trembling with exhaustion and the weight of defeat. Beneath the robe, his once-strong frame appeared thin and frail, his skin decayed from the venom. As the robe slipped from his shoulders, it revealed the full extent of his deterioration.

From seemingly nowhere, four blue Indian ringneck parakeets, crocheted like delicate amigurumi, flew into the hallway. Their tiny wings fluttered with determination as each gripped a part of Santa's robe with their talons.

The parakeets darted toward Darksant, fearless, as they released Santa's robe above him. Darksant grinned, spreading his arms wide as the robe floated down and magically cloaked itself around his towering form. The moment the robe touched him, its bright red hue twisted into a deep, dark mahogany, a shadow of its former self.

Darksant's grin grew wider, ear-to-ear, as black smoke swirled ominously around his hand and formed Santa's hat. He placed it atop his head, and instantly, a surge of dark energy rippled through his body, intensifying the aura of malevolence surrounding him.

"Finally," Darksant breathed, his voice dripping with dark triumph.

Darksant turned toward his throne, his voice dripping with cruelty. "Kill them all," he commanded his kobolds with a dismissive wave. "Be nice to Santa, though. He's already dying."

From behind the throne, the glowing eyes of the kobold army gleamed in the dim light, their grunts filled with anticipation as they eagerly awaited their dark master's orders.

Darksant paused, a mockingly thoughtful expression crossing his face. "Oh, how silly of me," he said with heavy sarcasm. "I almost forgot to wish you all..." He turned back to face Santa, Aiva, and Danta, his sinister grin stretching across his face like a sickening mask of delight. "Merry Christmas to all of you."

But before he could revel in the darkness of his victory, a sudden shout echoed through the chamber.

"Same to you!"

Tollbo leapt from the shadows, his war hammer raised high. With a furious roar, he swung it with all his might, the weapon smashing into Darksant's face with a resounding crack. The force of the blow sent Darksant flying across the room.

Santa, summoning every ounce of strength left in his weakened body, rose to his feet. With a surge of determination, he leapt toward Darksant, catching him mid-air as he fell from Tollbo's blow. In one swift motion, Santa seized the hat from Darksant's head. Without hesitation, Santa flipped Darksant over with surprising force, sending the dark sorcerer crashing into his own throne. The impact was so powerful that Darksant slumped to the floor, momentarily dazed, his malevolent smirk replaced by shock and confusion.

Santa, panting and trembling, stood tall. Though his body was decayed and covered in Darksant's venom, his spirit burned fiercely.

In that instant, the atmosphere in the room shifted. Tollbo moved quickly, freeing Aiva and Danta from their bonds. Santa, still catching his breath, approached Tollbo, his eyes wide with disbelief and relief. "I thought you were dead?" Santa asked, his voice trembling slightly.

Tollbo glanced at Santa and let out a chuckle. "In your dreams," he replied with a grin.

They both laughed, the tension in the room easing for a moment as they embraced.

The brief moment of camaraderie was shattered as Darksant rose to his feet. With a wave of his hand, he summoned his Kobold army, who assembled behind him, their eyes gleaming with malice. Darksant's eyes glowed with dark, evil energy, and his voice echoed through the chamber. "You think you can defeat me?" he sneered, his tone dripping with contempt.

Santa, Tollbo, Aiva, and Danta stood side by side, determination clear on their faces. Santa, though weakened, felt a surge of energy from the bravery of his friends. Tollbo tightened his grip on his war hammer, his eyes locked on Darksant with fierce resolve. Danta, though a little scared, showed a spark of fighting spirit as he clenched his fists. Aiva, more frightened than anyone, had her fingers numb and sweat running down her face.

"We have to protect the spirit of Christmas," Santa said, his voice steady.

"Together," Tollbo added, raising his war hammer.

Aiva and Danta nodded, ready to face whatever came next.

Darksant laughed, a cold, hollow sound. "Your courage is admirable but futile." With a wave of his hand, the Kobold army charged.

The battle was intense. Tollbo swung his war hammer with precision, each strike sending kobolds flying across the room. Danta fought with agility and determination, using his bare hands to smash plastic Kobold Barbie dolls, their pieces clattering to the floor. Aiva struggled at first, trying hard to fend off a gnome doll that jumped and kicked her in the face, causing her nose to bleed. But the pain only fuelled her anger. Furious, she stomped on the gnome doll, shattering it into pieces.

More gnome dolls approached, but Danta and Aiva teamed up, picking them up and hurling them against the wall. They tore apart cotton-stuffed dolls and puppets, their insides scattered across the floor as they fought with everything they had.

Despite his weakened state, Santa fought back with fierce determination. He kicked away the kobolds that ventured too close, even sneezing with such force that a nearby kobold was sent sprawling backwards. Each action was fueled by his desperate need to save Christmas.

Darksant's dark tentacles lashed out, aiming to ensnare Santa. With quick reflexes, Santa dodged the attacks and grabbed a large stuffed panda toy as a makeshift shield. The tentacles tore through the toy, sending cotton fluff swirling through the air.

At that moment, Tollbo charged at Darksant, his war hammer raised high. He leapt into the fray, but Darksant was quick to react, summoning his dark longsword to intercept Tollbo's strike. The two weapons clashed with a resounding explosion of metal, and they stood locked in a fierce struggle, neither willing to yield.

Meanwhile, back in Tollbo's igloo, Avnith sat alone, frustration simmering beneath the surface. A deep sense of self-doubt plagued him, causing him to question his worth as a brother. Sadness washed over him, heightening the loneliness he struggled with. In a sudden outburst, he kicked over the trunk, sending its contents spilling across the floor in disarray.

Amidst the scattered artefacts, his gaze was drawn to a small blue ball that had tumbled out of the pouch. The faint blue light emanating from it seemed to beckon him, sparking a flicker of curiosity amid his turmoil.

This time, there was no one to stop him. Avnith picked up the purple glowing ball and the pouch, examining its contents. He opened the pouch to reveal an array of blue-coloured balls inside, their purpose unclear. Holding one of the balls in his hand, he scrutinized it closely, half expecting it to be nothing more than a decoration. A wave of disappointment and sadness washed over him as he sank into a chair, the loneliness enveloping him once more.

As he sat there, the ball slipped from his grip and rolled a short distance across the floor. To his astonishment, a portal suddenly materialized where the ball had come to rest. Avnith's eyes widened in shock and awe as the portal opened, revealing the vacant interior of his home in Delhi.

Clutching the pouch tightly, he stepped through the portal and found himself back in his old surroundings. A sense of familiarity washed over him as he walked through his house, each step stirring a rush of emotions. He made his way up the narrow staircase to his small, cramped room. As he opened the door, a sudden gust of snowflakes swirled into the room, catching the light in a delicate dance. As the flakes settled, he saw—himself.

Avnith, just five years old and as thin as a reed, stood in the doorway of his new room. His small frame was barely visible against the dim light filtering through. The initial excitement he had felt about his new house had dissipated, leaving only a profound sense of disappointment etched across his face. His eyes, wide and forlorn, surveyed the small, cramped room before him.

Noticing his son's downcast expression, Avnith's father knelt beside him, his face a map of concern and empathy. "What happened, son?" he asked gently, his voice tender and soothing.

"It's small," young Avnith mumbled, his voice barely rising above a whisper as if the word itself carried the weight of his crushed hopes.

A tender smile softened his father's features as he reached out, brushing a stray lock of hair from Avnith's forehead. "Don't worry," he said softly, his voice imbued with warmth and reassurance. "It's temporary. When we build our own home, you'll have a big room, just like you want."

Young Avnith's innocent eyes, brimming with curiosity and uncertainty, turned up to meet his father's gaze. "Our home? This is not our home?"

His father's chuckle was gentle and comforting, a sound that seemed to wrap around them like a soft blanket. "This is our home too, son. Every place we live becomes our home, whether it's rented or built."

Young Avnith's small face scrunched up in confusion as he searched his father's eyes for clarity. "Then when can I call this my home?"

His father's smile deepened, and his love for his son was evident in the way he wrapped his arm around Avnith, pulling him close. "Home isn't about the size of the room or the type of house. Home is the people you live with, the ones you love. It doesn't matter if it's a tiny room in the city or a grand house in the mountains. What makes a home is the love and happiness we share with each other. As long as we are together, this—right here—is our home."

Young Avnith clung to his father, tears welling up in his eyes as he felt the comforting warmth of his father's embrace. The room, though small and unadorned, suddenly seemed to shimmer with a kind of magic he had never fully understood before. He buried his face in his father's shoulder, his tiny body trembling with a mix of relief and newfound understanding.

The teenage Avnith stood right in front of them, overwhelmed as he watched his childhood memory unfold before his eyes.

He stepped forward, reaching out as if to touch his father, but before he could make contact, the snowflakes swirled around the room once again.

As the snowfall settled, he found himself back in his small, humble room. The flashback had vanished, leaving him alone once more. The walls seemed to close in around him as his heart swelled with an overwhelming flood of emotion. The true weight of his father's message crashed over him like a tidal wave, engulfing every corner of his heart.

Avnith cried, overwhelmed by memories of the moments that had transformed their small house into a sanctuary of warmth and love.

He remembered the birthday celebration with Varshikha and Danta. Danta, grinning mischievously, had smeared a generous dollop of cake on Avnith's face. The laughter that followed was more than just sound; it was a warm, enveloping embrace that seemed to lift them above their everyday worries. Their joyous giggles echoed through the room.

He recalled another incident with the neighbor uncle, who was clutching a ball in his hand, fuming with anger as he pointed at the broken window. Avnith had stayed silent, taking the full brunt of the uncle's fury while Danta stood beside him, his small face etched with a mix of fear and admiration. Avnith had shielded his younger brother from the uncle's scolding, absorbing the reprimand meant for both of them.

Avnith's mind drifted to another poignant memory: it was 2 a.m., and he lay in bed with a high fever. The room was dimly lit, the only light coming from a small bedside lamp that cast a soft glow over his restless form. A damp cloth was placed on his forehead, a simple but earnest attempt to ease his discomfort.

Despite the late hour and her own exhaustion, Varshikha had refused to leave his side. She slept in a chair beside his bed, her silhouette a silent guardian against the darkness. When Avnith shivered with cold, she stirred, her face illuminated by a mix of fatigue and deep concern. Gently, she dipped the cloth into a bucket of cool water, her movements tender and precise as she wrung it out. With loving care, she placed the cloth back on his feverish forehead, her touch soothing and maternal.

Her hand, warm and steady, brushed through his hair, a gesture so simple yet profoundly comforting. In that quiet, feverish night, her presence was a sanctuary, her care a balm that spoke volumes without uttering a single word. The warmth of her touch and the soft rustle of her movements wrapped around Avnith like a protective cocoon, a silent testament to her unwavering love and devotion.

Avnith sank onto his bed, his fingers tightly clutching the pouch of emerald balls. The sense of longing and love for his family surged through him, mingling with a newfound resolve.

With a deep breath, Avnith stood up, ready to face whatever lay ahead with the strength of his newfound understanding.

Meanwhile, in Darksant's tower, the battle raged on. Santa and Tollbo fought side by side against the dark sorcerer. Santa, sweat pouring down his face, grumbled, "I wish I could wield my talwar."

Tollbo, swinging his war hammer with fierce determination, shot back, "Stop being a Bonehead. A true fighter doesn't need any weapon."

Santa's spirits lifted at Tollbo's words. He grinned and said, "Yeah, you're right, baby! Let's show him what we've got!"

Nearby, Aiva and Danta struggled with action figures, soldier dolls, monkey toys, and puppets that swarmed them. Despite being caged, Vini tried to motivate her siblings. "Come on, you can do it!" she yelled.

Darksant, sensing the momentum shifting, unleashed his dark tentacles, slapping away Tollbo and Santa and throwing them across the chamber.

A stretchy rubber snake toy wrapped around Aiva and Danta, making their movements stiff. Stuffed monkeys climbed into a cannon toy and hurled themselves at the children, kicking them and sending them flying. Aiva and Danta crashed beside the fallen Santa and Tollbo.

Darksant's tentacles snatched Santa's hat and placed it back on his head. "Now I will destroy you myself," he declared menacingly.

Danta, his voice unwavering, said, "I'm not afraid of you."

Vini, still caged but defiant, screamed, "Yeah, me too!"

Aiva, though a bit scared, "I'm, but I won't let you destroy Christmas."

Darksant dark tentacles spreading menacingly as he prepared to engulf the entire hallway in suffocating darkness. Just as the shadows began to close in, a sudden flash of blue light burst into the room. Two small portals opened around him, each crackling with energy.

From one portal, a pair of fists emerged, delivering powerful blows that sent Darksant staggering backwards. From another portal, the hat was snatched clean off his head, disappearing into the swirling blue void. As the sorcerer struggled to regain his footing, a third portal opened directly in front of Santa and his team.

With a burst of bravery, Avnith sprang from the swirling blue portal, clad in a cricket helmet and brandishing a bat. A duffle bag was slung over his shoulder.

Avnith quickly distributed the items: a cricket wicket to Danta, who accepted it with a nod of appreciation, and a badminton racket to Aiva, who frowned at the choice of weapon, clearly unimpressed.

Santa's eyes sparkled with a mixture of surprise and amusement as he took in the sight of Avnith's makeshift arsenal. Despite the gravity of the situation, he couldn't resist making a light-hearted quip. "Well, look at you, playing the hero and raiding a hardworking man's shop," he teased, his voice carrying a note of warmth and humour even amid the chaos.

Avnith, his resolve unyielding, handed Santa a baseball bat. "I had to come," he declared firmly. "You're my family."

Tollbo looked at Avnith incredulously, a puzzled expression crossing his face. "What? No, I'm not your family."

Santa, sensing the importance of the moment, gave Tollbo a sharp look. "Don't ruin this moment," he said gently. Tollbo glared at Avnith, his expression a mix of sternness and begrudging admiration. "So you went through my stuff and figured out how to use the portal balls," he said, his tone gruff.

Avnith, unflinching, met Tollbo's gaze. "You said I was a smart kid," he replied, a hint of pride in his voice.

Tollbo's frown softened into a reluctant smile. The tension eased, and the group, now unified and armed, turned their focus back to Darksant and his minions, ready for the battle ahead.

Tollbo, ready for action, said, "Let's fight again."

But Avnith raised a hand to stop him. "Wait a minute," he said, then shouted, "VINI!"

They heard her reply, "I'm coming!" A portal opened next to Avnith, and Vini jumped out, armoured with a skateboard helmet and pads and holding a racket.

Avnith smiled. "Now the team is complete."

They all charged at Darksant and his Kobold army. The battle resumed, filled with intense action and determination.

The battle raged on with fierce intensity. Santa, Tollbo, Avnith, Aiva, Vini, and Danta fought valiantly against the relentless kobold army. Every swing of their weapons, every fierce strike, rip, and stomp took down the tiny, malevolent creatures.

Avnith, weilding his cricket bat, fought valiantly alongside his team, knocking away toy soldiers and dolls. Vini, her eyes alight with determination, clutched her racket tightly as she faced Bhola and Chinya. Without hesitation, she swung her racket with all her might, sending the dolls flying across the chamber. The impact was satisfying, a resounding crack echoing through the air as Bhola and Chinya crashed into the wall and fell to the ground, motionless.

Aiva's badminton racket shattered as she struck the enormous 5-foot-tall stuffed panda doll. The panda, driven by wild, frenzied energy, lunged at her, sending her sprawling to the floor. As she struggled to get up, more 5-foot-tall stuffed pandas and teddy bears piled on top of her, their weight pressing down with crushing force. Her left arm remained visible, clawing desperately at the floor as she fought valiantly to free herself from the overwhelming pile of stuffed toys.

Nearby, Darksant's dark tentacles lashed out. Tollbo dodged the attack and retaliated by striking Darksant in the belly, sending him sprawling backward. Santa seized the opportunity, grabbing Darksant from behind, his fingers digging deep into Darksant's robe. With a powerful throw, Santa hurled Darksant away, causing the robe to slip from his body and tear apart. Darksant crashed into the wall with a resounding impact.

Santa quickly donned his robe again; the torn fabric magically mended itself as he wore it. However, amid the chaos, one of Darksant's tentacles snatched the hat from Santa's head, while another tentacle struck Santa, sending him flying across the room. In the midst of the turmoil, a spruce twig that had slipped from Santa's pocket skittered across the floor, coming to rest just within Aiva's desperate reach.

Aiva's fingers, stained and trembling, gripped the twig with a final burst of willpower. The twig transformed into a gleaming talwar, its blade igniting with a fiery orange light. With renewed strength, Aiva swung the talwar overhead, its edge slicing through the stuffed dolls with precise, furious strikes.

The imposing pile of kobolds was torn apart by the forceful blows of the talwar. As Aiva rose to her feet, bits of cotton from the shredded dolls fell around her like a gentle snowfall. The hallway was filled with the awe-inspiring sight of Aiva wielding the weapon with newfound grace and power. Her eyes, fierce and determined, reflected the blazing brilliance of the talwar, casting a radiant glow that matched her resolute spirit.

Santa and Danta, watching in amazement, couldn't help but smile with pride.

In a final, desperate surge, Darksant leapt towards them, his black tentacles flailing with dark, malevolent energy. His eyes glowed with a sinister light, the very embodiment of his dark magic.

Aiva, with fierce determination in her eyes, slashed through the air with the talwar, her blade slicing through the dark tentacles that reached out for her friends. The tentacles writhed and hissed as they were severed, their sinister grip broken by Aiva's precise strikes

Santa seized the moment, charging forward with all his strength. He tackled Darksant, gripping him by the neck with a vice-like hold. The force of Santa's grip seemed to pierce through the dark sorcerer's aura, causing Darksant's eyes to widen in shock and pain.

As Santa strained to maintain his grip, Tollbo let out a mighty roar and swung his war hammer. The war hammer's heavy, enchanted head struck Darksant's face with a thunderous crash. The impact was immense, sending Darksant reeling backward into a towering mound of fallen kobolds.

The dark sorcerer landed in a heap at the base of the pile, his body sprawled amidst the defeated toy soldiers and broken puppets. The once-menacing figure was now overwhelmed by the weight of his own darkness, his movements sluggish and defeated.

Santa and Tollbo stood side by side, their breaths heavy with exhaustion. The battle was not over, the kobolds began to reanimate, self-healing their dents and rejoining their stitches. Avnith, realising the dire situation, asked, "How do we kill kobolds?"

Tollbo responded with urgency, "Burn them!"

"How?" Avnith questioned, desperation in his voice.

Tollbo explained, "Portal balls are flammable." He and Santa grabbed a few portal balls, preparing to use them against Darksant. "Darksant will die if he gets out of this tower. Let's throw him out."

Santa, looking at the remaining portal balls, asked Tollbo, "How did you have so many of these?"

Tollbo, his voice sombre, replied, "They belonged to my 499 brothers who fought alongside me."

They hurled the portal balls at Darksant, whispering, "Out of the tower." Darksant, with agile movements, dodged the portals, leaping from wall to ceiling. He barely avoided being caught, evading with a sinister grace.

Avnith's heart pounded as he watched the mountain of kobolds, their eyes glowing menacingly as they prepared to launch another attack. Seeing the imminent danger, Tollbo quickly pulled out a portal ball. Avnith, with a determined glance, hurled the pouch towards the encroaching army of kobolds.

Chinya, ever alert and quick on her feet, spotted the pouch soaring through the air. She snatched it out of the air, her movements graceful and swift.

Tollbo, not wasting a moment, struck the portal ball with the head of his war hammer. The impact ignited the ball, causing it to burst into flames. He then hurled it with all his strength towards the Kobold. Bhola, who was standing imposingly above Chinya, grabbed the burning ball. The intense heat caused the Bhola's plastic arm to melt away. The molten arm fell with a clatter, landing on the pouch below.

In a brilliant explosion of bright blue flames, the portal ball detonated. The flames spread rapidly, engulfing the kobolds in a blazing inferno. The hallway was illuminated with a fiery glow, casting long shadows against the walls as the dark army was consumed by the flames. The once-menacing army was now reduced to a chaotic blaze of melting plastic and crackling fire.

Avnith shouted to Aiva, "Throw them out of the tower!"

Aiva, eyes alight with a better idea, grabbed her portal ball and whispered, "Into an active volcano." She threw it beneath the burning mountain of kobolds. The portal revealed a searing, churning sea of molten lava, its fiery surface bubbling and shifting with intense heat. The light from the lava cast a fierce orange glow across the chamber, illuminating the horrified faces of the kobolds.

One by one, the blazing figures of the kobolds were pulled into the inferno. Their frantic screams echoed through the chamber, mingling with the roar of the molten lava. As they plunged into the fiery abyss, the relentless tide of darkness was swallowed by the fiery chasm. The inferno consumed them entirely, leaving only the crackling remnants of their destructive presence. The chamber fell silent.

Bhola and Chinya clung desperately to the edge of the portal, their figures a grotesque mix of molten plastic and burning fury. They reached out with scorching, frantic hands toward Vini. With a determined cry, Vini swung her racket with all her strength. The impact sent Bhola and Chinya plummeting into the fiery depths of the volcano, their screams fading into the inferno. The portal slammed shut with a thunderous thud, sealing their fate.

Darksant unleashed his dark tentacles, shaping them into deadly daggers that he hurled at Santa and Tollbo. They barely managed to dodge a few, but some found their mark, causing them to groan in pain. With only 2 portal balls left, Santa warned, "Be careful. We only have two chances left."

The battle reached a fever pitch as the heroes launched the portal balls at Darksant. With remarkable agility, the dark sorcerer dodged their attacks, causing 2 portals to open on the floor. His dark tentacles surged out, aiming to ensnare the kids. But Aiva, with quick reflexes, slashed at the tentacles, sending them writhing back with a fierce swipe..

Tollbo leapt over Darksant, aiming to strike him, but the dark sorcerer was faster. He grabbed Tollbo by the neck and slammed him to the ground. Tollbo's head dangled dangerously close to one of the open portals, the wind whipping his long hair around his face.

Darksant exerted all his strength, trying to force Tollbo into the portal. Seeing this, Santa rushed forward to help. But Darksant was too quick, and with another arm, he seized Santa and pinned him in a separate portal.

As they were on the brink of being cast into the swirling void, Aiva appeared, her expression resolute and fierce. Wielding the talwar with precision, she moved swiftly and decisively. With a powerful swing, she cleaved through Darksant, splitting him in half. The dark sorcerer let out a guttural groan of agony as his body began to disintegrate into shadows.

The lower part of Darksant's body tumbled out of the portal.

Santa and Tollbo, freed from Darksant's grasp, sprang back as the portals sealed shut behind them. The immediate danger had passed.

Santa grabbed Darksant's upper body and struggled as his dark tentacles began to regenerate his lower half. Avnith shouted, "We're out of portal balls!" Darksant laughed sinisterly, "Foolish! You cannot kill me. My mission will succeed. The sun is rising, and you have failed!"

Tollbo, defiant, tore off his eye patch, revealing the portal ball embedded within his eye socket. He hurled it to the ground, opening another portal. Santa clung to Darksant, whose body had fully regenerated. *"Christmas ki hardik shubhkamnaye!"* Santa exclaimed as he loosened his grip.

Darksant plummeted into the portal, clinging to its edge. Tollbo swung his war hammer, shattering Darksant's grip. With a scream, Darksant tumbled out of the portal, falling from the night sky.

Darksant's black tentacles lashed out, ensnaring Vini and dragging her down alongside him. Without a moment's hesitation, Santa hurled himself after them. As they plummeted, the hat flew off Darksant's head. Santa seized the opportunity, grabbing the hat and placing it on his own head. Despite the strong force of the wind, the hat stayed firmly in place. The curse took immediate effect, freezing Darksant stiff in mid-air, his tentacles rigid and unmoving.

Santa deftly maneuvered around the frozen Darksant, his movements showing remarkable agility despite the peril. The final wave of Darksant's venom slithered over Santa's face, its dark, corrosive tendrils spreading across him. Clutching the unconscious Vini tightly, Santa descended rapidly, his robe billowing out like a makeshift parachute. Although the robe helped slow his fall, the weight of the venom dragged him down faster. The top of Darksant's tower loomed closer with each passing second. With a thunderous crash, Santa landed on the edge of the terrace.

Darksant's frozen body shattered into multiple dark fragments, some of which struck Santa with brutal impact. The impact was jarring, causing Santa to lose his balance and fall from the tower terrace. By sheer luck, Santa managed to grab the edge, holding on with all his remaining strength.

Just in time, Tollbo and the rest of the kids reached the tower terrace. They watched in horror as Santa, barely conscious, weakly handed Vini to Tollbo.

Tollbo took her protectively, his face etched with concern. The kids scrambled desperately to pull Santa up, gripping his arms and pulling with all their might. But Santa's strength was waning, his grip slipping. In a heart-stopping moment, Santa lost his hold and fell, disappearing into the darkness below.

The edge of the tower seemed to recede into the abyss as Santa plummeted, the rush of the wind roaring in his ears. The children's frantic cries echoed around him, their eyes wide with terror as they watched Santosh Chaube—Indian Santa—disappear from sight. Vini, still unconscious in Tollbo's arms, murmured weakly, 'Santa.'

Santa continued to fall, his eyes closed as the dark venom clung to him. But Vini's faint call pierced through the chaos, and his eyes snapped open. As if in response to her voice, the venom began to dissipate from his body. Miraculously, his wounds began to heal, the dark magic retreating from his form. With renewed strength, he grasped the tower's wall mid-fall.

Summoning all his remaining energy, Santa leapt back onto the terrace, landing with a firm thud beside the others. Relief washed over the children as they saw him stand tall, unharmed and rejuvenated. Santa's survival and miraculous recovery were nothing short of a Christmas miracle, and the air was filled with a collective gasp of awe and gratitude.

Santa grabbed Vini and blew gently over her face as snowflakes swirled around her. She stirred awake and asked timidly, 'Santa, are we alive?' Santa grinned mischievously and replied, 'You could always pull my beard to check.' Vini giggled and tugged on Santa's beard, and everyone burst into laughter.

CHAPTER 9

Homecoming

Snow began to fall gently from the sky, each flake drifting down like sifted white flour. The world around the tower transformed into a winter wonderland, with a soft blanket of snow covering the terrace in a pristine layer of white. Everything glistened under the delicate snowfall—peaceful and serene as if the night itself was blessing the moment.

Santa's sleigh stood ready atop the tower terrace, its polished frame gleaming under the soft light of the stars. The children, along with Tollbo and Santa, gathered around it, their breaths visible in the crisp, cold air.

Santa moved toward his faithful reindeer, his face softening into a warm smile. He patted each one with affection, his touch familiar and gentle. The bond between them was unspoken but deep, forged over years of countless journeys together. The reindeer responded with soft, affectionate nuzzles, their large eyes gleaming with the same warmth Santa had shown them.

Turning to his companions, Santa's heart swelled with a mix of pride and affection. The children had proven themselves brave, and Tollbo had been a steadfast companion. Now, they stood together, ready for the final leg of their journey.

"Are you ready?" Santa asked, his voice deep yet filled with warmth.

The children nodded, their faces glowing with a mix of awe and joy.

With a satisfied grin, Santa climbed into the sleigh, reins in hand. The reindeer stomped their hooves, eager to soar through the night sky. One by one, the children climbed into the sleigh, their faces glowing with anticipation. Tollbo hopped on, too, settling himself beside the kids with an exaggerated huff.

Santa gripped the reins firmly as the sleigh shot forward, the reindeer galloping toward the edge of the terrace. The world blurred as they reached the brink, and with a rush of wind, the sleigh leapt into the sky. Aiva's initial fear melted away, replaced by wide-eyed wonder, while Avnith's knuckles whitened as he gripped the edge of his seat, still uneasy with the dizzying heights. Danta and Vini, on the other hand, cheered with glee, enjoying the ride like an exhilarating amusement park thrill.

Tollbo managed to keep his usual grumpy face. The wind rushed past, carrying the cold bite of the night as Santa guided the sleigh higher into the night sky. They glided over Tollbo's igloo, a small glimmer of light far below. As Avnith glanced down, his heart tightened at the sight of the familiar landscape disappearing beneath them. A wave of nostalgia washed over him, but it was Tollbo who caught something in the distance.

His eyes narrowed, and there below was Teji—running, desperately trying to keep pace with the flying sleigh. The sight of the small figure growing smaller and smaller tugged at something deep within Tollbo. He sniffled quietly.

Avnith noticed and, without a word, placed a comforting hand on Tollbo's shoulder. They shared a quiet moment, a mutual understanding of the bittersweet farewell.

Santa glanced back at Tollbo from the front of the sleigh, his eyes twinkling as a teasing smile crept onto his face. "Tollbo," Santa asked with mock seriousness, "Are you crying?"

Tollbo quickly wiped his eyes, trying to hold onto his gruff demeanour. "No," he grumbled, his voice a little rougher than usual.

Santa, still smiling, tilted his head with a gentle look. "You can tell us, Tollbo," he said softly, inviting him to open up.

But Tollbo wasn't having it. With an impatient huff, he glared at Santa. "Push the damn button," Tollbo growled, clearly eager to shift the focus back to their journey.

Santa chuckled and hummed "Deck the Halls" under his breath as he reached for the red button. With a sharp push, the slot beneath the sleigh opened. Santa slipped on his steampunk glasses, then grasped the vintage-looking gear stick, pulling it smoothly.

With a loud THUNK!, two basketball-sized spheres shot out from the launcher, their radiant hues of red and green trailing like comet tails as they streaked toward the sky. The moment the spheres collided, they exploded into a dazzling spectacle of light, painting the heavens in shimmering colours. The glowing orbs expanded into an immense hyperdrive portal. Between those spirals, a vast vortex of liquid energy undulated, beckoning them forward.

The sleigh surged toward the portal, and with a thunderous WHOOSH! They entered the hyperdrive tunnel, hurtling through it at lightning speed. The children were transfixed by the sight—the tunnel around them was like an otherworldly aquarium filled with swirling nebulae, interstellar gases, and shimmering cosmic dust. They were flying through the galaxy itself. Time and space seemed to fold around them, making the journey both surreal and breathtaking. Tollbo, however, unfazed by the spectacle, yawned languidly.

Avnith, Aiva, Danta, and Vini stood, taking in the surreal surroundings enveloped by shimmering auroras. Aiva, turned to discover the opening hole of the hyperdrive tunnel had vanished, leaving only the endless tunnel behind.

Nevertheless, the sleigh continued its journey through the mesmerising tunnel, Santa's smile reflecting the joy of the moment. He cracked the reins again, and the sleigh accelerated, streaking through the celestial lights in a blur.

Ahead, a small bright dot grew larger and larger until—WHOOSH!—the sleigh emerged from the hyperdrive into the sky above Landour, Mussoorie. The transition was abrupt, the exit not as smooth as their entrance. The sleigh hurtled towards the Cedrus deodara forest, seemingly destined for a crash landing.

Yet, Santa reacted swiftly, pulling up on the reins just in time to clear the treetops. The reindeer flew over the canopy at great speed, manoeuvring with skill and agility. Finally, the sleigh descended towards Aiva's house, appearing to crash again, but Santa expertly guided it to a rough stop on the terrace.

Santa, his concern evident, glanced back at his passengers. "Is everyone fine?" he asked, his voice carrying a mix of worry and reassurance.

Avnith, looking tired but determined, nodded in response. Aiva, though dishevelled from the ride, managed a shaky but affirming nod. Danta, sprawled out on the seat, was breathing heavily but still showed signs of life beyond his exhaustion. Tollbo, unimpressed, yawned again, his boredom obvious despite the thrilling journey.

Vini, remarkably serene, wore a tranquil smile that belied her true condition. However, the facade quickly faltered as she suddenly retched, trying to conceal her discomfort. She clamped her mouth shut, desperate to keep her distress hidden from Santa and the others, her face flushed with the effort.

Later, as the excitement of their adventure settled into a warm glow of recovery, Avnith, Danta, Vini, and Aiva stood before Santa and Tollbo, their faces radiant with the joy of their extraordinary experience. Santa, his eyes twinkling with genuine warmth, addressed them with a broad smile.

"I promised you all that as soon as I got back, I'd complete my sleigh flying training," Santa said, his voice filled with hearty cheer.

Vini gently reminded Santa about the gifts. Santa's face lit up with a chuckle. "Right, that's why I'm here!" he exclaimed, a twinkle in his eye.

With a theatrical flourish, Santa reached into his magic pocket, his arm disappearing almost entirely into the enchanted fabric. When he pulled it out, he revealed a large red sack of gifts nearly twice his size. The sack was adorned with shimmering snowflakes and sparkling stars—an enchanting sight.

Santa placed the sack gently on the ground beside him. As he opened it, a soft glow illuminated the area, casting a warm light on the faces of the children, who watched with eager anticipation.

Santa began his gift-giving with a thoughtful gaze at Avnith, acknowledging the trials he had faced, the fears that plagued him, and the deep moments of loneliness. With a gentle smile, Santa handed Avnith an antique camera. Avnith looked at it, puzzled, the weight of its vintage frame heavy in his hands.

Santa encouraged him to look through the lens. With a trembling hand, Avnith peered into the camera, his breath catching as he saw something extraordinary. The lens revealed a moving bioscope of Avnith's past—a series of cherished memories featuring his deceased father and mother. In one scene, young Avnith sat on his father's shoulders, his mother beside them, holding balloons. The memory shifted to his father hugging him tightly and sharing the real meaning of home, a moment Avnith had almost forgotten.

The film continued with a scene from his childhood: Avnith lying in bed, unable to sleep, while his father played a lullaby on his guitar and his mother ran her fingers through his hair. Eventually, Avnith drifted off to sleep. His father wrote down the lullaby on a piece of paper and tucked it under Avnith's pillow. His mother then kissed his forehead and tucked him into bed. Together, they watched him sleep peacefully, a moment of pure love and tenderness unfolding before Avnith's eyes.

Overwhelmed, tears welled up in Avnith's eyes, his chest tightening with emotion. He turned to Santa, his voice catching as he tried to express his gratitude. Santa, with a gentle smile, placed a comforting hand on Avnith's shoulder and softly shushed him.

"These are your memories," Santa said soothingly. "Keep them safe."

Avnith nodded, clutching the camera, feeling an immense sense of closure and warmth. The gift was more than just a camera—it was a bridge to his past, a precious connection to his parents that would always remain with him.

Santa's eyes twinkled as he called out to Danta, who stood with barely contained excitement, his curiosity palpable.

"Danta," Santa began with a warm smile, "your name means 'Calm,' just like one of the names of Lord Hanuman.

But you remind me of him only as a child—full of mischief. So I have a special gift for you, one that will help you channel your energy into something positive: knowledge."

"This," Santa continued, presenting the scroll with a flourish, "is the Yahgo Scroll. It's no ordinary scroll. Whatever question you have, whatever mystery you wish to unravel, this scroll will write the answer for you. It holds knowledge that even Yahoo and Google couldn't provide."

Danta's eyes widened in amazement. He gingerly took the scroll from Santa's hands, his mind racing with the endless possibilities of what he could discover with such a powerful tool.

"Thank you, Santa!" Danta exclaimed, his voice brimming with gratitude.

Santa chuckled warmly, patting Danta's shoulder. "You're very welcome, Danta. Use it wisely, and may it bring you the answers and adventures you seek."

Danta nodded vigorously, his face alight with excitement.

Then, it was Aiva's turn. Santa turned to her with a warm, approving smile. "Aiva," he began, "you have shown remarkable courage and strength. It's not easy to find a gift for someone as brave as you."

Aiva stood tall, though a hint of uncertainty flickered in her eyes. Santa pondered for a moment, then reached into his pocket and pulled out his spruce twig.

"This," Santa began again, but Aiva hesitated, unsure if she was worthy of such a significant gift. "Are you sure I can take this?" she asked, her voice tinged with doubt.

Santa nodded, his eyes twinkling. "This is a symbol of your courage and the strength you've shown. Take it, Aiva. I hope you never need to use it, but it belongs to you now. Only the chosen can wield this spruce twig, and it has chosen you."

With newfound confidence, Aiva reached out and took the spruce twig from Santa's hand. The moment her fingers closed around it, she felt a surge of warmth and power, as if the twig itself was acknowledging her worthiness.

"Thank you," Aiva said, her voice steady and filled with determination. She held the spruce twig close, knowing that it was more than just a gift.

Finally, Santa knelt before Vini, his expression tender and full of affection. His voice was gentle as he began, "Thank you for making such a wonderful wish."

Santa's praise was heartfelt and sincere. "Because of your belief, we found Tollbo and defeated Darksant. In a world where belief in Santa is fading, it's rare to find someone like you. Your faith and spirit keep the magic of Christmas alive. Vini, your heart is so pure. You have a light within you, a spark of wonder and joy more powerful than any gift I could ever bring."

Santa's voice became more impassioned. "You have the courage that many adults can learn from. You faced dangers and stood up for what was right without losing your innocence or your smile. Do you know how special that makes you?"

Santa's eyes shimmered with unshed tears as he gazed at Vini, his voice thick with emotion. "Every year, I deliver gifts, and for so long, it's just been a regular job for me," he said, his words heavy with the weight of countless Christmases past. "But because of you, Vini… you've reminded me that my job is not just a job. It's so much more."

He paused, taking in the warmth and innocence radiating from her, a gentle smile tugging at the corners of his mouth. "Thank you, Vini. Your belief fuels my sleigh, your joy gives my reindeer the strength to fly, and your kindness fills my sack with gifts of love. Never underestimate the power of your belief, Vini. It is the very essence of Christmas magic."

The children around them listened in awe, their eyes wide with wonder and admiration.

Vini looked up at Santa with wide, innocent eyes and said, "What? I didn't understand. You said too many things!" Her voice filled with genuine confusion.

Everyone around them chuckled warmly. Santa's eyes twinkled with amusement "Never mind," Reaching into his pocket, he pulled out a delicate snowflake pendant. He placed it gently around Vini's neck.

"This pendant is special," Santa explained. "When it glows red, it means I'm nearby. If it glows green, it means there's danger around you."

Vini furrowed her brow, trying to make sense of this new information. "But my teacher said red means danger and green means safe," she said, her small voice serious.

Santa looked momentarily puzzled and glanced at Tollbo, who simply shrugged, his expression saying, "I don't know."

Santa chuckled, the sound warm and reassuring. "Don't listen to your teacher. From now on, green means danger, and red means Santa," he clarified, his tone playful yet sincere.

Vini nodded enthusiastically, delighted with her new pendant and the playful confusion of its colours. She held it close, feeling its warmth and the magic it represented.

Avnith, Aiva, Danta, and Vini stood side by side, their eyes reflecting the twinkling lights of the night sky. Each held their special gifts close.. Santa, his face glowing with pride and love, looked at each child, his heart swelling with the joy of the season.

Santa's eyes glistened with emotion as the time to say goodbye approached. He looked at the children, his voice soft and filled with warmth. "Hug me, please."

The kids rushed forward, wrapping their arms around him in a heartfelt embrace. Santa's hearty laughter rumbled through the cold night air. "I hate goodbyes," he murmured, holding them close.

Tollbo, standing a few steps away, cleared his throat, breaking the bittersweet moment. "Goodbye reminds me... how's my wife, Vulpi?"

Santa looked momentarily lostbut quickly regained his composure. "Oh, she is doing well. I mean, she's alive and well," he assured.

Tollbo's eyes narrowed, but he continued, "And my son?"

Santa's face brightened with genuine pride. "Thospow is following in your footsteps. He's brave and strong, just like you."

For the first time, a genuine smile spread across Tollbo's gruff face. The two friends exchanged a nod of understanding.

They both turned back to the children, the moment of departure upon them.

Danta looked up at the horizon, worry creasing his brow. "Santa," he said, his voice tinged with concern, "the sun is about to come up in half an hour. How will you deliver all the gifts in time?" As he spoke, the Yahgo scroll, clutched in his fingers, began to glow with a radiant white light. Danta's mouth fell open in shock as he witnessed the magic unfolding before his eyes.

Santa threw his head back and laughed, "Kid, I'm Santa Claus. It takes me ten minutes, tops, to deliver all the gifts in India."

The children exchanged amazed glances. Santa tucked the giant gift sack into his magical pocket and, with Tollbo, climbed back onto the sleigh. Santa winked at them, the twinkle in his eye even brighter.

"Christmas ki Hardik Shubhkamnaye!" Santa exclaimed.

Vini, Danta, and Tollbo looked puzzled, while Aiva and Avnith clarified, "It's Santosh Chaube style." The children echoed, "Christmas ki Hardik Shubhkamnaye!"

Tollbo made a grumpy face and grumbled, "I say Merry Christmas." He wished the children a Merry Christmas, and they responded warmly.

Tollbo then turned to Santa. "Now, let's move."

Santa cracked the reins, and with a final wave, the sleigh lifted off, soaring into the night sky. The children watched in wonder, their hearts full of memories, as the sleigh ascended higher and higher. The reindeer galloped through the starry expanse, their hooves dancing in the air.

With a final, brilliant flash, the sleigh disappeared into the portal, leaving behind a trail of sparkling stardust.

The children stood in silence, the weight of the adventure settling over them like a warm blanket. They had fought bravely, loved deeply, and believed with all their hearts. In that belief, they had saved Christmas.

CHAPTER 10

Merry Christmas

The children stepped back into the house, their hearts still warm from their magical adventure. Inside, chaos awaited them—furniture was overturned, and decorations were scattered everywhere. The once-festive home looked as if it had been through a storm.

Avnith, Danta, Aiva, and Vini exchanged determined glances. This house, their home, needed to be restored to its former glory. With a shared sense of purpose, they rolled up their sleeves and got to work. Avnith, who had once been reluctant to celebrate Christmas, now led the charge with newfound energy, directing the others as they picked up broken ornaments and righted the furniture.

Vini, exhausted from the night's events, tried to help but soon found herself drifting off to sleep on the couch, her hand clutching her snowflake pendant. The others worked quietly around her, careful not to disturb her well-earned rest.

Piece by piece, the house began to transform. Danta found some tinsel and draped it over the furniture, while Aiva carefully placed ornaments back on the tree. Avnith moved like a whirlwind, hanging lights and setting up the nativity scene with a joy that was contagious. By the time the sun had fully risen, the house was not just clean but beautifully decorated for Christmas.

Outside, the sound of a car pulling into the driveway caught their attention. Avnith peeked out the window and saw Abby and Varshikha returning home. Abby was in a wheelchair, her foot wrapped in a plaster cast, with Varshikha gently guiding her up the snowy path to the front door.

The door swung open, and both mothers stepped inside, their eyes widening in surprise. The house, which they had left in such disarray, was now a winter wonderland. Lights twinkled, the tree sparkled with ornaments, and a sense of warmth and festivity filled the air.

"Wow," Abby whispered, her voice filled with awe. "What happened here?"

Varshikha looked around, equally amazed. "It's beautiful! You kids did an amazing job."

Avnith, Aiva, and Danta stood proudly in front of the decorated Christmas tree, their faces lit with wide smiles. The room sparkled with festive cheer, illuminated by twinkling lights and colourful ornaments adorning the tree.

It was the perfect Christmas morning surprise for Abby and Varshikha. The hard work and love the children had put into decorating had transformed the space into a winter wonderland, making the holiday even more special.

Later that night, the house was filled with the sounds of laughter and celebration. The Christmas tree stood proudly in the corner, its lights twinkling softly. Outside, the gentle snowfall created a serene contrast to the warmth within.

Danta, his excitement still lingering, hurried over to his mother, Varshikha, holding his scroll as if it were the most precious thing in the world.

"Mom, look at this!" he exclaimed, his eyes wide with wonder. "It's a magical scroll. You can ask it anything, and it will write the answer!"

Varshikha smiled down at her son,. "That's wonderful, Danta," she said, her voice warm and encouraging. "Why don't you show me how it works?"

Danta nodded eagerly, his small hands gripping the scroll tightly as he closed his eyes in concentration. "What's the best way to make a perfect snowman?" he asked, his voice filled with anticipation.

But when he opened his eyes, the scroll remained blank. His face fell slightly, and confusion creased his brow. He gave the scroll a little shake, hoping to coax an answer from it, but the parchment stayed stubbornly empty.

Varshikha watched him with a gentle expression, sensing his disappointment. She reached out and softly patted his shoulder, her touch reassuring. "It's okay, Danta," she said soothingly. "Why don't you help me serve the guests for now? We can always try again later."

Danta looked up at her, still feeling a bit puzzled by the scroll's silence. Reluctantly, he nodded and followed her to the kitchen, tucking the scroll into his pants as if it were a fragile treasure.

Moments later, Avnith, now dressed in his finest suit, descended the stairs and joined the party. His appearance drew appreciative glances from the guests, and he moved through the crowd with a confident stride, greeting everyone with a warm smile and soaking in the joy of the evening. As he made his way closer to the kitchen, Varshikha approached with a tray of cold drinks. Her gentle smile illuminated her face as she asked, "Do you need anything, Avnith?"

Avnith shook his head. "No."

Varshikha was about to turn away, but Avnith hesitated, then called after her, "Wait."

She stopped, a look of confusion crossing her face as she turned back to him. "Yes, tell me, beta."

Avnith took a deep breath, gathering his thoughts. He had been carrying the weight of his feelings for so long, and now, in this moment of peace, he knew he had to let them out.

"I've been unfair to you," he began, his voice trembling slightly. "I've blamed you for everything—for my father's death, for the emptiness I felt after he was gone. Every time I looked at you, I saw the life I lost, the happiness I thought was taken from me."

Varshikha's eyes softened, but she remained silent, allowing him to continue.

"But I realise now," Avnith said, his voice growing stronger, "that I was just trying to find someone to blame. It was easier to put it on you than to face the truth. I was lying to myself, using my anger to hide how much I missed him. And in all that time, I was too blind to see what was right in front of me."

His eyes glistened with unshed tears as he looked at her. "I was remembering my parents during hard times, thinking I was all alone. But I was a fool. Because I already had someone who cared for me, who was there for me even when I pushed her away. I already had you."

Varshikha's breath caught in her throat. She had waited so long to hear those wordsand to see this side of Avnith. Her heart swelled with emotion, and she could barely contain the tears that welled up in her eyes.

"Avnith..." she whispered, her voice thick with emotion.

"I'm sorry," Avnith said, his voice cracking. "I'm sorry for every time I hurt you, for every harsh word, for every time I made you feel like you didn't belong. You've done nothing but try to give me a home, and I've been too stubborn to accept it. But I see it now."

Varshikha set down the tray and stepped closer to Avnith, her hands trembling as she reached out to touch his face. Her tears finally spilled over, and she smiled through them, her heart aching with both sorrow and joy.

"Welcome home," she said softly.

"Merry Christmas, Mom," he whispered.

Varshikha's tears flowed freely now, but they were tears of happiness, relief, and finally being accepted. She held him close, her heart full to bursting.

"Merry Christmas, Beta," she replied, her voice choked with emotion. "Thank you... thank you for this gift."

They stood there for a long moment, mother and son, finally united in love and understanding.

As the party continued, Avnith's gaze swept through the room until it settled on Aiva. She looked stunning in her purple gown, a vision of grace and beauty. Gathering his courage, he made his way toward her.

"You look beautiful," Avnith said, a genuine smile lighting up his face.

Aiva smiled back, her eyes sparkling with warmth. "And you look very handsome."

For a moment, they stood there, simply savoring the quiet connection between them. The room around them seemed to dissolve, leaving only the two of them in that serene moment of understanding. Then, Avnith spoke softly, "Merry Christmas, Aiva."

Aiva's smile flickered as she reached into her pocket, pulling out a small, folded piece of paper. It was carefully taped back together. Nervousness tinged her voice as she handed it to Avnith.

"This is for you," she said, her voice trembling slightly.

Avnith took the paper, his heart pounding with anticipation. "Is this…?" he began.

With trembling hands, Avnith carefully unfolded the paper. It was the lullaby his father had written for him—a melody composed during a time when he struggled to fall asleep, a heartfelt symbol of his father's love and care. As he read the familiar words, a flood of emotions surged within him. A gentle smile spread across his face, and a warm sense of comfort enveloped him, connecting him once more to his cherished memories.

Aiva watched Avnith, her eyes filled with regret. Her voice trembled as she spoke, "I never threw it away. I lied when I said the wind blew it out of the window. The truth is, I wanted to get back at you. I taped it back together and tried many times to return it, but every time we met, we ended up fighting. In my anger, I wanted you to feel the hurt I did. I'm sorry. I've been wrong."

He looked up at Aiva, his eyes misting over. "Don't be sorry. We all have that bad person inside us. I confronted mine, and you confronted yours. Thank you," he whispered.

Avnith reached into his pocket and pulled out another folded piece of paper. He handed it to Aiva with a shy smile.

She looked at him, confused.

Aiva unfolded the paper, her eyes scanning the handwritten lyrics. As she read, her emotions swelled with each line. Her eyes widened with a mix of surprise and gratitude as she looked up at him.

"It's about me," she said, her voice barely above a whisper.

Avnith nodded, a gentle smile on his lips.

"This… this is the most valuable gift anyone has ever given me," she whispered, her voice filled with happiness.

Avnith smiled, his heart brimming with warmth. "I'm sorry it's not more," he said softly.

Aiva's eyes glistened, not with tears but with joy. Without saying another word, she hugged him tightly, and he hugged her back just as fiercely. It was a moment of healing, where old wounds began to mend and new promises were made.

In the distance, Varshikha and Abby watched their son and daughter reconcile. Varshika, still in disbelief, turned to Abby and asked, "How is this happening?"

Abby smiled warmly, handing Varshikha a slice of cake with a cherry on top. "With a cake of belief and a Christmas cherry on top," she said, her eyes twinkling with joy.

Vini, her eyes sparkling with excitement, darted through the crowd of guests, heading straight for her mother, Abby.

"Mom, you won't believe what happened last night!" Vini exclaimed, bouncing on her toes with energy. "We fought Darksant, and Santa gave me this magical pendant! It glows red when he's nearby and green when there's danger! And he told me not to listen to the teacher!"

Abby smiled indulgently at her daughter. "That sounds like a wonderful dream, sweetheart," she said softly, her voice filled with warmth.

"But Mom, it wasn't a dream!" Vini insisted, holding up the snowflake-shaped pendant for her mother to see. "Santa really gave me this!"

Abby nodded, her eyes flicking to the pendant with a gentle smile. Just then, a guest approached to greet Abby with a warm "Merry Christmas." Abby shook hands with the guests and greeted them with a cheerful "Merry Christmas." She paused for a moment, turning her gaze toward Vini, a thoughtful expression on her face.

" Vini," Abby said, her tone affectionate. "Why don't you show it to your friends?"

Vini pouted slightly, feeling a little deflated, but the excitement in her heart couldn't be diminished. She quickly ran off, eager to share her magical story with her friends.

As she ran through the room, her pendant suddenly began to glow a vibrant red. Vini stopped in her tracks, startled, and glanced down at the glowing pendant. Her eyes widened with a mix of surprise and wonder. She turned slowly and looked out the nearby window.

There, just outside the window, Vini spotted a familiar, bulging eye peeking through the frosted glass. It was unmistakably DD. A knowing smile spread across Vini's face, and without hesitation, she waved at the eye, her heart fluttering with excitement.

With a mischievous glint in her eye, Vini took a deep breath and blew a raspberry at DD. The eye blinked in surprise, a hint of amusement shimmering in its reflection.

Suddenly, her friends came rushing toward her, drawn by her laughter and eager to join in. As they approached, DD quickly retreated into the sky, vanishing as swiftly as it had appeared.

Santa's sleigh was parked high above the clouds, where the stars shimmered in a way that made the whole sky seem to be smiling. DD retreated through the clouds, zipping straight into Santa's waiting arms. With a fond smile, Santa tucked DD back into his magic pocket. "Damn, I love kids," Santa murmured, his heart swelling with warmth.

Tollbo sat beside Santa on the sleigh, his gaze falling on the soft, contented smile that lit up Santa's face. He couldn't help but comment, "Feeling lucky, Santosh?" His tone was gruff but it carried an undercurrent of tenderness.

Santa nodded, "More than ever. This has been the best Christmas of my life."

Tollbo nodded, but his thoughtful expression revealed a lingering concern. Santa noticed his unease and asked, "What's on your mind?"

Tollbo hesitated before speaking. "Everyone knows the dwarf-elves never lose a war. Yet 500 of our bravest fought against Darksant and became martyrs. How did these children—just children—manage to defeat him?"

Santa smiled warmly, his eyes twinkling with a knowing light. "Sometimes, you must realize that even in the darkest moments, everything holds a little miracle... and magic."

Tollbo grunted in agreement, a sound that was more affectionate than anything else. With a sly grin, he reached under his coat and pulled out a couple of beer potions and two tankards. "Well then, let's celebrate! A toast to the best Christmas ever."

Santa hesitated, eyeing the tankards with a mix of amusement and caution. "Oh, I don't know, Tollbo. I usually don't..."

Tollbo cut him off with a grin, shoving a tankard into his hand. "Take it as medicine," he quipped, his eyes gleaming with mischief.

Santa laughed, a hearty sound that echoed through the quiet sky. "Alright, alright. Just for medicine."

Tollbo uncorked the beer potions and poured them into the tankards, the rich, frothy liquid bubbling up as the two friends prepared to toast. They raised their tankards high, ready to celebrate the perfect night, but just as they were about to clink them together, a distant wail of police sirens reached their ears.

Startled, both Santa and Tollbo froze, their tankards hovering in mid-air. In a split second, they tossed the beer over the side of the sleigh and hid the tankards behind their seats, their hearts pounding with a sudden rush of adrenaline.

Santa, visibly irritated, muttered under his breath, "Damn, CPD." Tollbo, always quick on his feet, nudged him gently and whispered, "Play it cool."

A sudden flash of red and blue lights cut through the night's tranquility like a beacon, illuminating the clouds with a vibrant glow. Santa and Tollbo stood frozen as a figure came into view. It was Inspector Dumper, a portly man dressed in a uniform that was as festive as it was authoritative. His badge, marked 'CPD - CHRISTMAS POLICE DEPARTMENT,' sparkled with twinkling lights and tiny jingling bells. His sunglasses gleamed with the reflection of the stars, and his name badge, 'Inspector Dumper Dunker Rangela,' shone brightly.

Inspector Dumper was astride his police hover bike, a marvel of festive engineering known as "HUH! SN-342."The hover bike combined the sleekness of a chopper motorcycle with the magic of a flying broomstick. Its frame floated effortlessly in the air, lacking traditional wheels but equipped with a soft, glowing aura that made it seem as if it were suspended by enchantment. The front featured a large, warm headlight, while the siren atop flashed vibrant red and blue lights, casting a captivating dance of colors across the night sky.

Santa and Tollbo, standing on their sleigh, were momentarily frozen, their hands raised high in the air like suspects caught red-handed. The flashing lights danced across their faces, illuminating the surprised expressions they wore.

Inspector Dumper, ever the professional, set down his half-eaten doughnut on the tray beside him and reached for his megaphone. With a voice that was both authoritative and laced with holiday cheer, he announced, "Santosh Chaube, batch number 420. Sleigh no. 9-2-11. Indian Santa Claus. Arctic Circle City founder and our beloved St. Nicholas has invited you and General Tollbo to his palace for a private Christmas party."

Santa and Tollbo erupted in joy, their eyes lighting up with pure, unbridled excitement. They exchanged gleeful looks like children on Christmas morning. Inspector Dumper, watching them with a hint of envy, sighed softly to himself, "When will I get a chance?"

Santa wasted no time. He leapt into his sleigh seat, gripping the reins with resolute determination. The reindeer,

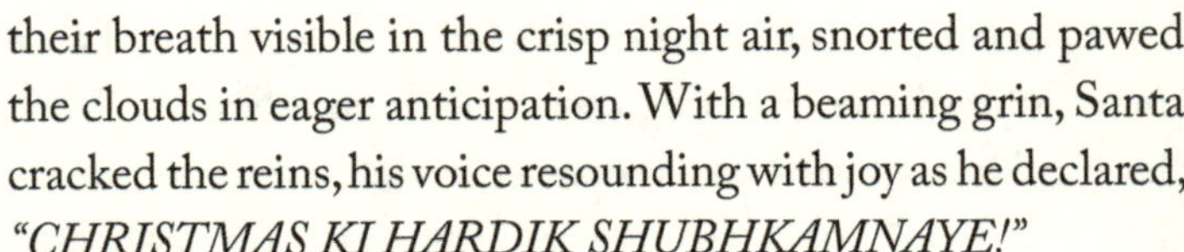

their breath visible in the crisp night air, snorted and pawed the clouds in eager anticipation. With a beaming grin, Santa cracked the reins, his voice resounding with joy as he declared, *"CHRISTMAS KI HARDIK SHUBHKAMNAYE!"*

In an instant, the sleigh surged forward, rocketing into the night sky with a burst of exhilarating speed. The clouds parted like curtains unveiling a grand stage, revealing a vast expanse of stars that glittered like diamonds scattered across a velvety canvas. With a brilliant flash and a whoosh, the sleigh was swallowed by the shimmering embrace of magical hyperdrive.

The sleigh vanished, leaving behind a trail of glistening stardust. The stardust mingled with the falling snowflakes, creating a mesmerizing dance of glittering light that gently cascaded upon the world below, like a final magical blessing for the night.

The adventure had come to an end, but its magic lingered, a reminder that the spirit of Christmas was alive and well in the hearts of those who believed. No more evil would threaten Christmas—at least, not for now.

But…

Evil is like a shadow cast by the brightest light—it never truly fades. It lurks, waiting, reshaping itself, unbound by time. For every darkness that is vanquished, another waits to rise. The harsh truth is that evil cannot be so easily vanquished. It adapts, it festers, and when it returns, it comes back stronger and more cunning.

Far from the warmth of celebration, back at Darksant's tower, a sinister stirring began.

Teji, the Himalayan Tahr and Tollbo's only companion for all those years approached cautiously, his nostrils flaring as he sniffed the ground. His breath misted in the cold air as he drew closer, unaware of the dark presence slowly gathering around him.

The pieces of Darksant's frozen body scattered across the rocky surface began to vibrate with a low, unsettling hum. Thick, black fluid seeped from the shattered fragments, oozing and merging together. Gradually, the fluid coalesced into a grotesque form—a dark sea urchin, initially the size of a small seed, pulsating with malevolent tentacles.

Teji, frozen in terror, watched as the creature's dark tendrils surged toward him with horrifying speed. The tendrils wrapped around his head, twisting and constricting with dreadful strength. Teji's frantic bleats echoed through the desolate landscape as he fought desperately against the nightmarish creature. But his struggles only seemed to tighten the urchin's grip, each movement further entwining the black tendrils around him.

Teji, once a powerful, large goat, now struggled to rise on his hooves. He grew weaker, his bleats fading into desperate gurgles as darkness consumed him. His trembling body finally came to a stop, lifeless. The malevolent urchin drained the life from him, and as his body lay still, dark fluid mixed with blood seeped from his nostrils. The fluid merged and expanded, reforming the dark urchin, now larger than Teji's head. It screeched with bone-chilling intensity, a harbinger of its return and a terrifying warning to the world that evil had returned.

To be continued…

"Christmas ki Hardik Shubhkamnaye."

www.ingramcontent.com/pod-product-compliance
Lightning Source LLC
La Vergne TN
LVHW091056150826
845673LV00002B/606

* 9 7 9 8 8 9 5 4 4 5 4 7 1 *